THE NUTCRACKER CURSE

Cursed Fairy Tale Book 1

MARGO RYERKERK

❧ 1 ❧

GRISELDA

Sunrays streamed through the tiny bars of the prison window. The other prisoners rushed toward the light, bathing in its warmth and gazing longingly out the window and onto the azure sea that surrounded Snake Island.

I didn't join them. Instead, I remained in my position on the cold stone floor and pulled out my magic mirror from my enchanted bag, which was invisible to everyone but me. Focusing on the mirror, a keepsake from my dead mother, I willed it to show me what was happening at Schönbrunn Palace, the summer residence of the Austrian emperor and his daughter, Crown Princess Clara. Painfully slow seconds trickled by as the mirror continued to show me my own reflection until, finally, the surface rippled like waves in the ocean. My face disappeared to be replaced by *her* face.

I consciously loosened my jaw before my teeth grinding ended with a chipped tooth. I hated her. I hated everything about my stepsister. I hated Clara's oval face that looked more refined than my square one. Her blue eyes that were so much brighter than my gray ones could ever be. Her long, gold-brown tresses that were thick and voluminous and never hung limply on her shoulders, unlike my dull, ash brown hair. She was wearing a satin gown tied at her back, revealing her feminine curves, curves that my flat body lacked. The dress wouldn't suit me, and yet, I longed to rip it off her, put it on, and stuff her in my brown, stained prison garb.

I should have been living in the palace, walking around in beautiful dresses. Instead, I had been banished to Snake Island a month after I had turned eight because of Clara. If she hadn't run her stupid mouth and told my stepfather, the king, that I had dark magic that allowed me to shift into a mouse, he would've never banished me. I would've continued being his stepdaughter, and Mother would still be alive and ruling by his side.

Because of Clara, I was stuck here while she frolicked in the palace. Watching my stepsister running down the stone corridor and chitchatting with the help made disgust rise in me. She shouldn't be talking to the servants. She should be in the study, crafting war strategies and arranging allegiances, making the kingdom stronger as a real crown princess would. Clara didn't deserve the title. It should be mine, and soon it would be.

From underneath my cloak, I pulled out the white-bearded nutcracker dressed in a red-and-black soldier uniform, black boots, a tall hat, and a silver sword attached to his belt. After working on him for the last year, the time had come to use him.

As if on cue, Clara exclaimed, "Really, my fairy godmother is coming as well? How wonderful!" She clapped her hands together, as if she were still seven and not seventeen, and I had to subdue my gag reflex.

The nutcracker in my hands had been a gift to Clara from her dead mother, and the only item I had been able to swipe before I had been banned from the palace and forced to live on this forsaken island. At first, I had wanted to destroy the wooden doll, but fortunately I had resisted. Now, the nutcracker would become the tool to facilitate my revenge and help me reclaim my kingdom.

In addition to mouse shifting, my mother had passed on the ability to perform dark spells, which had manifested a year ago when I had turned seventeen. For a year, I had been working on a spell for the nutcracker, and finally, it was ready. I touched the wooden figure, not worried that I would unleash the curse I had placed within. The curse wouldn't attach itself to just anyone—it was specifically designed for Clara. Unfortunately, like all curses, the Nutcracker Curse wasn't infallible. Magic required that each curse could be solved. However, the solution to the curse was nearly impossible to obtain, and I wasn't worried about Clara or anyone else from the dimwitted Austrian Empire succeeding.

I examined the figurine one last time, then checked on the fist-sized, blue-lit orb. The circular light was a portal, crafted by a talented witch who had secretly copied the main portal in the chief of the guards' office. Both portals connected our island to the various kingdoms we had been banished from. The portal was only big enough to allow small items, such as letters to pass through. I had tried before to shift into my mouse form and slip through the passage, but it had sensed my presence and that I was a being, not a thing, and rejected me.

Each day for a year now, I had been using my dark magic on the portal, making it less resistant. It was still too strong and unyielding to permit me passage; however, in less than forty-eight hours and with a final boost of magic from me, it would let through an inanimate object bigger and heavier than a letter—the nutcracker.

Using my powers for both the curse within the figurine and to widen the portal had cost me a lot of energy and depleted my dark magic reserves for the foreseeable future.

Not ideal, but a necessary sacrifice. Because once the nutcracker traveled through the portal, it would end up in Schönbrunn palace and eventually find its way into Clara's curious hands, making her pay for revealing me as a shifter to the emperor.

❧ 2 ❧

CLARA

As I strode down the plush, ruby carpet, I was certain somebody was spying on me, but when I whipped around, I only found crystal chandeliers and gilded walls behind me. I sighed. For a year now, I'd had the feeling that someone was watching me, intending ill will. The sensation would come and go, lasting only for a few minutes. Each time, no one was there. Was I going insane? I shook my head vehemently, banishing the scary possibility and telling myself I was just overly cautious. And how couldn't I be when my governess, Bernadette, constantly reminded me to sit straight, not to fidget, and never ever yawn in public, assuring me in her low alto voice that even when I was certain I was alone, somebody was always watching me, the heir of the Austrian Empire.

Thinking of Bernadette reminded me I needed to go to my dance class. I glanced at my pocket watch and cringed. It was ten past twelve, and I was once again late for my lesson. Worse, I wasn't wearing my dancing slippers, but my favorite ankle boots with a sturdy one-inch heel that allowed me to walk fast and even run, two activities Bernadette didn't approve of.

Cursing the current fashion, which dictated multiple layers of petticoats, I picked up my skirts and dashed down the marble corridors toward the mirrored ballroom.

Out of breath, I reached the big wooden double doors to realize the guard on duty was my dear friend Philip.

"You're late." With a grin, Philip opened the doors for me. His forest-green eyes roamed over my disheveled appearance without judgment, while I noticed with envy that his skin had turned a golden shade from the spring sunshine. Unlike me, Philip could do in his free time as he pleased, not having to worry about getting color that was unbecoming for a princess.

"I lost track of time," I confessed as I slipped past him into the vast ballroom. The parquet floor shined, the chandeliers sparkled, and Bernadette glared at me.

"I'm glad you deigned to show up to your lesson, Your Highness," she said in a dry tone. Even though she was plump and, in her fifties, her spine was straight, her shoulders were pulled back and down, and her stomach was sucked in. Compared to her, I was a sloven.

Immediately, I stood straighter and put the sweetest smile on my face. "I apologize, but I'm here now, and I'm very excited to learn the...." I tried to remember what I was supposed to be learning today, but for the life of me couldn't.

"The *loure*, a *danses à deux,* a partner dance you will be performing at your coming-of-age ball. As you might recall, last time we learned the basic steps." Bernadette shot me a sharp look, daring me to admit that I had already forgotten the sequence of the dance steps. "Today, we'll dive into the more complex patterns."

"Why can't we do the polka?" The fast and upbeat dance always brought a smile to my face and never made me yawn.

"Because we're learning a traditional, classical dance, not some fad."

"It's been popular since at least 1840. Is ten years a fad?"

Bernadette ignored my comment and nodded at the white-haired piano player, who fell into a serene, slow melody.

For the next hour, I tried to memorize as many steps as possible, stay with the rhythm of the music, and not trample all over the feet of my partner, a middle-aged man with a permanently serious expression.

When the tower clock chimed one, I glanced at Bernadette expectantly. "Are we done?"

Bernadette crossed her arms. "We're staying here until you get the steps right."

"But what about lunch?" I asked, my stomach choosing this moment to growl.

Bernadette shook her head disapprovingly, as if I could control the noises my stomach made and simply chose not to, then said, "We're not leaving until you learn the *loure*. Your coming-of-age ball is tomorrow night, and it must be perfect. Otherwise, how do you expect any of the visiting princes to propose to you?"

I don't. I'm not ready to marry. I didn't voice my thoughts, knowing that doing so would get me nowhere with Bernadette and that if she relayed my inappropriate words to Father, he would be deeply disappointed. I couldn't do that to him. I was all he had left.

In a chipper voice, Bernadette continued, "You're of the right age to get married. Many girls in other kingdoms marry as early as fifteen. Your father agreed to postpone your coming-of-age ball until you turned seventeen due to my recommendation that you needed more time to learn everything a princess needs to know given your... restless nature."

I pressed my lips together to stop myself from saying that

it wasn't my fault I was the only available heir. I wasn't being difficult on purpose or to disappoint Father. My personality was simply not suited for the role I was supposed to fill. And I was nowhere ready to marry and rule Austria. I needed more time.

"Now, now, don't look so glum." Bernadette handed me a glass of water and rang the bell for the maid. "Please bring us some sandwiches and cookies."

Even chocolate chip cookies didn't cheer me up, but I was grateful Bernadette had sent for them, instead of making me feel guilty for not being excited about marriage.

Busy trying to process how much my life might change in the next few days and how I could avoid an engagement, I didn't complain during the next few hours as Bernadette made me repeat the steps over and over again until everything was perfect and the dance sequence was burned into my mind. By the time we were done, the sun was low in the sky. I considered going to Father's study but decided I needed some time alone to clear my mind and figure out how to talk him into giving me an extension, or at least a long engagement of two or three years.

Since I always did my best thinking outdoors, I exited the castle and went to the stables. I bypassed the horses, which neighed in protest as they were used to me bringing them carrots and spending a few minutes petting them and brushing their hair. But today, I didn't have time to say hello to everyone; I needed the comfort of Biscuit.

Biscuit had the biggest stall at the end of the stable. Her big, brown eyes met mine. There was so much depth in them, I felt as if she understood me. As always, she was an immaculate shade of white, like fresh snow. Her horn glinted as rays of sunlight touched it, giving it a translucent, ice-like quality. Biscuit used to be my mother's unicorn. The magic in her blood meant she had a much longer life expectancy than a regular horse and might even be immortal. Nobody knew, since unicorns weren't native to Austria, and my mother had brought Biscuit from Ireland.

"Hey, girl." I petted Biscuit's thick mane, which was the color of liquid, white gold. "Are you up for a ride? I could really use one." I saddled her and was walking her out of the stable when Philip came rushing toward me. A guard had replaced him at the entry to the ballroom earlier, so I hadn't talked to him since Bernadette's lesson. Even without me saying anything, he must have sensed something was wrong from my posture, because he said, "I'll come with you." Not waiting for my reply, he grabbed his inky stallion, Ace, and saddled him.

For a few minutes, we rode in silence. How I wished I always felt the way I did in the saddle—free, without responsibilities I wasn't equipped to fulfill weighing heavily on me.

Philip tore me back to the present. "You should have asked for an escort. You shouldn't be out riding alone, especially this close to sunset."

I shrugged. "There's a lot of things I'm not supposed to do."

"Was Bernadette hard on you for being tardy?"

A mirthless laugh spilled from my lips. "Bernadette is the least of my worries."

"Then what is it? Talk to me."

"The coming-of-age ball. I'm not ready to meet my future spouse." The words tasted like steel, hard and disgusting. If it weren't for Father, I would run away, but I couldn't do that to him and completely shatter his already fractured heart.

Next to me, Philip stiffened. For a while, we rode in silence until I couldn't take it any longer. "I'll talk to Father, ask for an extension."

"You must marry eventually." Philip's voice broke, and I studied him. His chin was as strong as always, his cheekbones

9

sharp, and his eyelashes sooty, but there was so much pain on his face. I reached out to touch his forearm, but he moved his horse away from me.

"A marriage won't separate us," I said. "We'll still be friends. As the heir, I won't leave. Whoever will become my spouse will move to Vienna."

I tried imagining myself in a white wedding dress, smiling at my future spouse, but couldn't. Instead, an image of another wedding popped into my mind. I was four years old and holding my new stepsister's hand, as a heavy, golden crown was placed on her mother's head. An overpowering floral musky scent hung in the air. The fabric of my dress itched. And my throat was parched. Even back then, I hadn't been comfortable with my stepmother. I knew something was off about Jacqueline, and when I had been seven, she had proved me right.

I rolled my shoulders, willing the past to leave me alone. My gaze landed on Philip, who no longer looked dejected but fierce as a muscle in his jaw ticked.

"What is it?" I asked.

He gave a sharp shake of his head. "Nothing."

I rolled my eyes. "Please, we've known each other since we were kids." Our bond was special, forged by our common loss. My mother had passed away giving birth to me, and Philip's mother, one of our royal seamstresses, had succumbed to a respiratory disease when he had been twelve.

"Fine. You want me to spell it out, then I will." Philip's green eyes turned on me, drilling past my title and my manners, or lack of them, to the person I was underneath.

The intensity in his gaze made me want to break eye contact and run. The tingling sensation roiling through me was too much, too strange, and I didn't know what to do with it or what it meant.

"I want what's best for you, and I don't want any of those foreign princes to take advantage of you or Austria."

My heart softened, and I put my palm on his hand. This time, he didn't pull away; instead, he studied my skin, as if memorizing the mole above my little finger and the fine lines on my hand.

"I won't let anyone take advantage of me. I promise. I won't allow anyone to sweet talk me into anything or sway me with good looks and charm."

Philip nodded, but the doubt remained on his face.

I paused, trying to come up with a way to put him at ease. An idea popped into my head, and I snapped my fingers. "I'll invent a test for the princes. Only those who pass can court me, and I'll insist to Father that I want to be courted for an extended period before getting engaged." That way I would get the time I needed without disappointing Father.

Philip mustered a weak smile that didn't reach his eyes, and I glanced away. Neither of us wanted me to get betrothed and have a husband stand between us. I couldn't bear the idea that once I became a wife, my friendship with Philip would have to take a back seat and that the freedom I had so carefully carved out for myself would be ripped from me.

❦ 3 ❧

CLARA

"Father, please, let's put off the engagement until I turn eighteen," I pleaded, having failed to convince him that my coming-of-age ball should be just a way for me to meet the other princes, not look for a spouse.

Father shook his balding head. "I'm getting older, Clara. I need to make sure that when I'm gone, the kingdom is taken care of. You need a spouse to rule with you, a strong and smart consort by your side."

"You're not going anywhere soon," I protested, trying to ignore the new wrinkles that had wormed themselves onto Father's forehead and his droopy eyelids that were becoming heavier with every day.

Father gave me a soft look. "Not yet, Clara. But illnesses are unpredictable; they strike us when we least expect it. It would take several years for somebody to learn everything about our kingdom. I want your husband to have time to acquaint himself with our customs, our land, and our people, instead of being thrust into rulership."

I nibbled on my lip, something I always did when I thought, and something that Bernadette hated, as I considered how I could spin Father's concerns to convince him to give me leeway.

"All right. But I need time to make the right choice. It's important to find the right spouse."

Father raised a bushy eyebrow. Before he could protest, I continued. "Everybody can be charming at balls. You said so yourself, you want a good spouse for me who would also be a good ruler, which means we need to evaluate the princes in a regular setting, not during a ball when it's a child's game to appear pleasant and fun. Make the princes study up on our history and economics, test them to see whether they're any good at it. And allow me to get to know them and find out who is kind and who is here just for power and our gold."

I held my breath as Father mulled over my proposal. Finally, he nodded slowly. "This is a smart strategy. As long as you know, Clara, that eventually you will have to pick one."

Because I wasn't enough. I wasn't a strategist made to rule the kingdom. I wasn't the son Father should have had. If only my birth had been easier, and Mother's recovery hadn't taken a turn for the worse. If only she could've given Father the male heir he craved and needed.

Pushing my aching pain down, I said, "I understand. Please give me a year before announcing my engagement."

Father scratched his beard. "Are you trying to scare away your suitors? Most of them are traveling here with the intention to stay a month or two, not twelve."

I jutted out my chin. "Is that so? Do we really want someone who doesn't think I, and the kingdom, are worth investing time and effort into?" Was I such a mess that I needed to be married off as soon as possible?

Father chortled. "Very well, you clever girl. You shall have three months before we announce your engagement." I opened my mouth to protest, but Father held up his hand. "That's long enough. Trust me. I know what's best for you."

Father pulled me into a hug, and I hugged him back, trying not to wriggle as his cobalt wool coat embroidered with golden threads scratched my arms. "Now go and prepare for the ball."

I left Father's study, trying to tell myself that three months was plenty of time to make a decision and that I could insist on a long engagement. And then what? How long would it take until my spouse demanded that I become one of those boring and regal royals who never raised their voice, laughed, or ran? I didn't want to be kept in a cage—a pretty ornament and nothing more.

Tramping down the marble halls extra loudly, my gaze fell on an abandoned toy.

I picked up the wooden cat, wondering what child at court had dropped it. It was just a toy, and yet handling it created a tight sensation in my chest as memories of my step-sister overwhelmed me.

"Let's play tea!" Griselda exclaimed, skipping down the stairs. She and her mother had moved into the castle a few years prior, and while I always had the urge to hide behind a curtain or underneath a table when Jacqueline's dark gaze fell on me, I always sought out Griselda, the sister I thought I'd never have after Mother's death.

Griselda and I darted through the playroom door, and I arranged our guests, stuffed animals and wooden toys, around the table while Griselda prepared the miniature silver tea set.

Our maid, Iris, brought us a plate of cheese and grapes to snack on. But I ignored the food, too busy brushing the hair of my new doll that I had received for my seventh birthday.

"Clara! Clara!" Griselda's voice had turned shrill, and when I looked up, I found that her nose was twitching in a strange way, her shoulders were hunched forward, and her hands were brought close together like I had seen a squirrel do.

"Are you all right?"

She didn't reply. Her eyes were glued to the plate of food, and then she charged and snatched up a piece of cheese with her mouth, not bothering to use her hands.

"Griselda! What are you doing?" Worried by my sister's odd behavior, I rang the bell for Iris.

Griselda dropped to the ground and convulsed, her limbs twitching. Terrified for her and of her, I kept my distance until Iris entered.

"You called, Your Highness?"

"Yes, Griselda—" Before I could finish my sentence, Griselda let out a piercing yelp, and her body vanished into thin air. A mouse crawled out from underneath her dress and darted across the room.

"A mouse! A mouse!" Iris shrieked as I quickly grabbed the plate cover and caught the rodent.

We called for Father, who thought we had made up the story and that Griselda was simply hiding somewhere. The guards were sent to search the castle and its perimeter. They returned empty-handed just as my stepmother arrived from a carriage ride. I was in the midst of retelling what had happened when the plate cover trembled, then flew across the room to reveal Griselda, who sat in a crouched position. Her ears were round and gray like a mouse's, and she had a tail and whiskers, but the rest of her body was human and, thankfully, it remained clothed in the dress she had worn that day. Her mouse-like features disappeared within seconds, but it was too late. Everyone in the room had seen her transform.

"She's a shifter," Iris whispered.

"Unholy, dark magic." A junior guard made the sign of the cross.

"We need to lock her up. She's a danger to the crown princess," another guard said.

Father stared at Jacqueline, his nostrils flaring. "You're a mouse shifter?"

Jacqueline didn't reply with words. One moment she stood by the door, the next her hands closed around my neck hard, cutting off my circulation. The guards tore her off me and handcuffed her, as well as Griselda.

Father's body vibrated with wrath. "Throw them both into the dungeon. In separate cells. I don't want them to hatch any ungodly magic together."

My body quivered. What had I done? How could I have betrayed my sister?

"Your Highness." The guard in front of my room bowed and opened the door. I blinked away the memory and entered my chambers, not feeling in the least excited about getting ready for the ball.

My maid, Iris, was already in my dressing room, ironing out the last few creases on my lilac dress adorned with silk flowers. It had a skirt big enough for four young children to hide underneath and see-through shoulder cap sleeves, which would highlight my collarbone and arms.

"Perfect timing, Your Highness. Your dress is ready." Iris undid the binding at the back of my day dress, and I stepped into my evening gown. She laced up the brocade dress tightly, giving me a wasp waist and making it hard to breathe.

"Thank you, Iris," I said after she curled my hair and put it in an updo, and applied powder, rouge, and eye makeup to my face.

She smiled at me kindly. "Is there anything else I can do for you, Your Highness?"

I bit my lip, unsure if I should share what was on my mind. But Iris had always been so calm and understanding that I decided to share my worries. "Do you ever wonder how Griselda is doing?"

All color drained from Iris's face, and her fingers shook. "No. It was a relief when she left."

Seeing how much my question had upset her, I didn't press further. "Why don't you take the evening off, Iris? You look tired."

"I'm fine, Your Highness."

The dark circles underneath her eyes and her stooped shoulders told a different story. "Please, Iris. I insist."

"Thank you, Your Highness." She curtsied, her old bones giving a creak that made her lower her eyes, as if her age was something to be ashamed of. I watched her leave, hoping I wouldn't lose her. Iris had guided me through the death of my mother, had watched me grow up, and now with all the changes coming my way, I needed her more than ever.

As my guards escorted me to the ballroom, I felt a stare to my left. I turned that way to find nothing but a landscape painting on the wall. Was it all in my head? Was I imagining that someone was watching me? Or was something more sinister at work, like dark magic?

❧ 4 ❧

CLARA

My worrisome thoughts vanished as the guards paused in front of the gilded double doors to the ballroom. A trumpet screeched inside, and the announcer boomed in a baritone voice, "Her Royal Highness, Clara Marie of Austria." The court cheered, and the heavy wooden doors opened. I was momentarily blinded by the bright chandeliers hanging from the angel-muraled ceiling and the polished mirrors that reflected the court and me a hundred times, creating a luscious sea of fine dresses and extravagant jewels. The long dining tables had been decorated with satin linens and cream-colored roses. Fine china plates depicting lovely birds and flowers were surrounded by gold flatware.

Father's eyes sparked with approval, and my shoulders dropped with relief. I crossed the room and joined him at the dais, taking the throne seat to his left side. "My beautiful daughter, you look like an empress." He squeezed my hand, and I took a sip of my water to counteract the sudden dryness of my mouth. Was that what Father hoped for me, that I would look the part of the empress without actually ruling? Did he think me completely incompetent and had given up on me?

To prevent myself from getting lost in dark thoughts, I distracted myself by surveying the room and smiling and nodding at several courtiers who I considered friends. I hoped I would get the chance to enjoy the ball and dance with them before the foreign princes arrived, but only minutes later, the trumpet buzzed again.

I took a deep breath, telling myself to stay optimistic. Perhaps one of the princes would understand me. Perhaps my soulmate was out there. Someone who would want to learn and grow together as rulers.

The announcer peered over his glasses at the thick scroll in his hands. "Prince Simon of Bulgaria." Simon was almost a head shorter than most of the guards, and as he bowed to my father, fat rolls became visible underneath his fuchsia jacket. He kissed my hand, his lips moist and warm, his own hand clammy. His rapid blinking told me he found the situation even more unnerving than I did. While this realization relaxed me, meeting Simon also created a new fear. Until now, I had been so concerned with losing my freedom through marriage that I hadn't even considered what my choices in a spouse would be like. Automatically, I had assumed that all princes would be good-looking, charming, and kind.

Father would never be so cruel as to wed me to a man twice my age, but Simon was not someone I was attracted to. I couldn't imagine kissing his lips, which were twice the size of mine, let alone marrying him. I doubted we had much in common when most of my pastimes involved being active, while Simon's first move after being seated was to inhale two liver canapes in one bite.

When the trumpet sounded again, my stomach tingled, and I hoped the second candidate would be better. "Prince Julian of Bohemia."

The second prince wasn't overweight; in fact, he didn't have an ounce of fat anywhere that I could see. His tall and lanky frame meant I had to strain my neck to make eye contact with him as he strode toward me. His lips barely grazed my skin as he kissed my hand, and he didn't crack a hint of a smile as he said, "I'm looking forward to discussing with you the future of the Austrian Empire."

He took his assigned place and didn't touch his food or take a sip from his wine. Instead, he scanned the room, as if studying and measuring all attendants. When his gaze fixed on me, I had the overwhelming urge to fidget, feeling as if he knew all my mishaps, all the times I had been late for my classes. Could he tell that I was impulsive, that I constantly got into trouble? I thought so, and I was certain he disapproved.

"Prince Felix of Serbia," the announcer called, and I focused on the third prince strolling toward me. A smile tugged at the corners of my mouth. That was more like it. Felix was a few inches taller than my five foot five. He wasn't overly skinny or obese, and seemed neither sluggish like Simon, nor scrupulous like Julian.

"I'm honored to be here, Your Majesty." Felix bowed to my father then kissed my hand, holding it a little bit too tight, but not painfully so. "I'm looking forward to getting to know you better, Princess Clara."

"Me too," I replied truthfully. I studied Felix as he took his seat amongst the two other princes, relieved that he neither scarfed down his food and wine nor ignored them. His gaze wandered across the ballroom in an appreciative manner, not a judging and analyzing one.

The trumpets sounded for what I knew was the last time, eliciting relief and trepidation in me. I was eager for the formalities to be over, but I also hoped that the fourth prince was promising.

"Prince Leon of Romania."

There was a collective sharp intake of breath, and several ladies picked up the speed of their fanning. I didn't follow suit, even though the temperature appeared to have risen a few degrees. Prince Felix could've been considered handsome, but Prince Leon was stunning. His long mane of blond hair was slicked back to reveal a face that seemed to have been carefully carved out of marble to create perfect symmetry. He was a head taller than me, the ideal height, and his muscles were visible through his clothing.

He gave a wide smile to Father. "I'm so glad I finally get to meet you, Majesty, and your beautiful daughter, Clara." As he kissed my hand, he didn't break eye contact, his blue eyes glinting with mischief.

I hated to admit it, but I immediately felt a pull toward Leon. It was impossible to stay immune to his good looks, but it was more than that. From the four princes, he was the one I could imagine making me laugh and sneaking off with into the gardens for some fresh air. Well, at least until I noticed Philip's scowl. The other guards didn't seem fazed, but my friend was clearly unimpressed with Prince Leon. Did he have a good reason? Or did he simply dislike sharing the attention of the court? I had overheard, on more than one occasion, several ladies saying that Philip was the best-looking guard and how it was a pity that he wasn't a duke or at least a baron.

I didn't share their sadness. To me, Philip was perfect just the way he was. He didn't need money or to speak four languages to be interesting or intelligent. Despite no formal education, he often surprised me by presenting well-thought-out views on politics and economic matters.

The trumpet sounded again, tearing me out of my thoughts and into the present. It was time for me to show off my *loure* skills.

To not display any favoritism, I had to dance with each prince in the order of their arrival. The idea of touching Simon's sweaty hands made me cringe; however, I saw no way out. Just because there was no way I would marry him, didn't mean I could be rude and risk making an enemy out of him.

"Your coming-of-age ball is delightful," he said as he led me onto the gleaming dance floor. The orchestra started a slow melody, and we shuffled awkwardly. Simon's steps were always a bit too slow, his jumps half as high as mine, and I had to spin carefully to not bump into his elbow. Uncaring about any of this, he kept up a cheerful stream of chitchat. "The music is excellent, and so is the food and drink. The clams are heavenly."

I managed a weak smile. "I'm glad you are enjoying them."

Simon continued to tell me about other dishes he liked, but I didn't catch most of what he was saying because I was facing the door where Philip was positioned. To anyone else, he would've appeared stoic, the perfect guard, but I could read the amusement in his eyes. I could only imagine what he thought about uncoordinated Simon. Having my friend there to share my opinion about how unsuitable the prince of Bulgaria was made my steps bouncier and my body relax.

When the dance ended, I discreetly wiped my hands on my dress, wishing I could wash them. Unfortunately, I didn't even manage to take a sip of water before Julian strode up to me. His dance steps were precise, and he didn't make any mistakes or miss a beat. However, he lacked fluidity, and his movements were wooden, as if we were marching, not dancing. He kept two feet's distance between us, making me want to sniff myself to ensure I didn't stink.

"So, what are your plans for the kingdom? Where do you see it in five and ten years?"

"Those are great questions," I stalled, unsure how to reply.

So far, I hadn't needed to worry about my kingdom's future. Father grew the kingdom's strengths and ironed out its weaknesses while I focused on my studies.

"I suppose it all depends on various factors," I said slowly. "How other kingdoms are doing and what the crop is in a given year." I thought, for an answer on the spot, mine was pretty good, but, clearly, Julian didn't share my belief.

"You must have strict rules in place and ensure your subordinates follow them, otherwise there will be pandemonium." On this joyful note, the song ended, and I curtsied, an icky bitterness coating the inside of my mouth.

"Are you having a fabulous time?" Felix asked as our dance started. Not giving me a chance to reply, he continued, "Of course you are. You're wearing the most expensive dress here, and no cost was spared for your coming-of-age ball." His tone held wonder and a hint of jealousy... No, that couldn't be, could it? Was that what Felix saw when he looked at my court —their wealth? If so, what did he see when he looked at me? I decided that I needed to do some digging into the state of his kingdom and proceed with caution. I had no interest in being married to somebody who valued foremost my money.

Even before my dance with Felix was over, Leon caught my eye, winking at me. As soon as he could swoop in without being rude, he did. His hands rested confidently on my shoulder and waist, and his lips were only inches away from mine. His every move was smooth, like his body was designed for dancing, and together we glided across the dance floor.

"Where did you learn to dance like this?" I asked as he twirled me.

He winked. "My court likes entertainment, and as their prince, I see fit to give them what they want. I throw balls at least weekly." He leaned in and whispered in my ear, "And I plan to give you, darling Clara, what you desire." He pulled back and looked at me earnestly. "I want you to be happy with me. I don't want to be your second choice. If there's anything you ever need, please, tell me."

"Thank you. That is very considerate of you." I was slightly taken aback by his intensity, but then again, what did I know? No one had ever dared to pursue me, knowing that only a prince would do. I had no experience with what was normal in courting. Perhaps Leon's passion was the ideal way to court someone. After all, his looks were phenomenal, his behavior was charming, and his dancing was superb. It only made sense that his courting too was of the highest caliber.

As the dance ended, I saw out of the corner of my eye, Felix hurrying toward me. After all the twirling, I really needed to grab a bite and have a sip of water, so I stormed off the dance floor as ladylike as possible. However, Felix was quicker. I was a foot away from my table when his hand touched my shoulder. "Could I have another dance, Princess Clara?"

I turned around slowly, trying to figure out the best way to tell him that I needed a break without offending him. No words left my mouth, because just then a shrill, discordant bell blasted. The jarring sound was the opposite of the friendly sound of the trumpet announcing a visitor. The high-pitched bell meant danger, and I wasn't the only one disturbed by the sound. The courtiers inched toward the walls, glancing around nervously and whispering in hushed tones while half of the guards stormed out of the ballroom to investigate the alarm.

Before I could find out what danger we faced, an elderly woman in a charcoal cloak poofed into appearance next to me. She pulled down the hood to reveal flowing silver hair and a deep frown on her face.

"Fairy Godmother, what is going on?" I asked, grateful to

see my guardian angel, but also worried since she only got involved when I was in trouble.

"The castle's security has been breached," she answered calmly.

❦ 5 ❦

CLARA

My heart pounded. "Are we under attack from another kingdom?"

Godmother shook her head. "No, the alarm you heard is only activated when dark magic breaches the castle."

Father nodded and turned to the herald. "Tell everyone that there is no reason for panic, but that the festivities are concluded for tonight and will resume tomorrow. They will be notified when and where."

As the announcer repeated Father's words, I searched for Philip in vain. He was no longer in the ballroom, and my gut clenched. Philip was always the person who wanted to protect everyone. If he found the foreign magic, I was certain he would try to disable it himself. I wanted to run after him, tell him to be cautious, but couldn't. Father took my elbow and ushered me into his study, which was the most secure location in the palace. Despite his and my fairy godmother's presence, my insides roiled with unease.

When it was just the three of us, Father asked, "Can you sense whose magic passed through our portal?"

"It's Griselda's magic. The trace is the same as her mother's," Godmother replied.

Dark spots danced in front of my vision, and I had to grip the desk for balance. "But Griselda is locked up on Snake Island, far away from here."

Father clenched his fists, and I remembered his fury the day my stepsister had turned into a mouse. As terrifying as that had been, she hadn't done it on purpose or to scare us. She had inherited from her mother, Jacqueline, shapeshifting, which was considered dark and unholy sorcery, and had no control over her powers, her instincts triggered by the cheese plate.

Her mother's actions, on the other hand, had been calculated. Jacqueline had chosen to attack me after I had inadvertently revealed her daughter's secret. She wanted to hurt me.

Tearing myself back to the present, I realized no one had answered my question. "Is Griselda no longer in the prison at Snake Island? Did she break out?"

"I haven't received any news of an escape." Father ground his jaw.

Godmother sighed. "Just because she isn't physically here, doesn't mean she's not a danger to you."

"I don't understand."

Ignoring my question, Father pointed a finger at Godmother. "You promised you would keep Griselda and her devilish magic away from my daughter."

Godmother lifted her chin. "I did all I could. I told you from the start that the protection spell I put on Clara wouldn't last her whole lifetime, but rather only ten years until she would be ready to face Griselda's magic."

I hugged myself. "How? I don't have magic of my own."

A vein popped on Father's forehead, and his nostrils flared. "Does Clara look like she's ready to face evil magic?"

"You don't need magic to fight dark magic," Godmother replied cryptically.

I inhaled deeply, trying to stop the lightheadedness and dizziness that threatened to overcome me. Ever since Griselda had been sent away, Father had never lost his temper. Him doing so now, showed me how dire the situation was. "What can Griselda's magic do to me?" My voice sounded weak and far away.

Once again, my question was ignored as Father murmured underneath his breath, "I should have executed the pup with her mother."

Godmother shook her head. "No. That wouldn't have been right. We didn't know whether Griselda would try to attack Clara in the future or not."

I touched Godmother's cloak sleeve, fighting the tenseness in my chest. "If your protection spell has expired and Griselda's magic is here, I really need to know how I can protect myself against her. I need you to tell me everything."

She nodded. "You're right, my child. Let me begin at the start. After the death of your mother, your father was looking for a wife and a mother for you and met Jacqueline. Everything about her seemed perfect. She was polite, friendly, beautiful, and intelligent. And she managed to cloak her magic, so that I had no idea what she was." She paused. "Not all shapeshifters and magic-users are bad. Unfortunately, your stepmother used her abilities for nefarious purposes, including putting your father under a love spell, which only broke when he saw you in danger."

Father stared out of the window, his hands clasped behind his back, and my heart ached for him. It must've been horrible to realize that he had been tricked into love and marriage.

"It was easy for Jacqueline to hide her magic in the palace since I was the only one who could've noticed it, and my visits were rare and brief. However, what Jacqueline couldn't control was her growing daughter. I believe she expected her daughter to come into her powers much later and was surprised by her shifting for the first time at age eight.

"Jacqueline sealed her and her daughter's fate when she attacked you in her rage, revealing her true colors. Since Griselda had inherited dark magic but hadn't used it for nefarious purposes yet, she wasn't executed but sent away to the prison on Snake Island. There was no way to strip her of the magic she had inherited, thus, I put a protection spell on you, which would last for ten years, but begin to wear off after nine years."

Godmother paused, and a realization overcame me. "I've had the feeling that someone was watching me for a year now. Could it be Griselda?"

Godmother nodded. "I'm afraid so."

"Why don't you just redo the protection spell?" Father asked in a terse voice.

"I can't. I'm sorry, but this is not how it works. Clara is of age now. She must stand up to Griselda."

"How do I protect myself from Griselda's magic, and what exactly can she do to me?" I asked, not liking the concern shining in Godmother's eyes.

"First, we need to understand what Griselda wants. My guess is that she will try to avenge her mother, perhaps even try to claim the throne."

"Clara is the only rightful heir! No mouse shifter will ever rule Austria!" Father brought his fist down on the table, spilling a vial of ink.

"Can her magic hurt me from Snake Island?" I chewed my lip until I tasted blood.

Father rang the bell. "I'll send guards to Snake Island at once, and they'll ensure she won't be in a state to use her magic."

I cringed at Father's words and the implication that Griselda would be tortured. While I understood his intention was to protect me, I couldn't stand back and allow him to torment a girl who was in prison due to her mother's actions and being born a mouse shifter.

"There must be a better way."

Godmother took my hands. "You have such a big heart, Clara. And yes, there is another way, but it isn't easy."

"What do I need to do?"

"Face Griselda and overcome her darkness with your goodness."

I swallowed hard. "How would I do that?"

"You won't!" My father dragged me away from Godmother. "Don't you dare fill Clara's head with such nonsense! Non-magic users will never win against magic users." Anger emanated from him, and I knew there was no point in arguing with him. Thus, I didn't voice my thoughts, namely, that while I had no magic, my unicorn Biscuit did, and that there might be magic users in our kingdom who could help me prepare to face Griselda.

While I mulled this over, Father instructed the captain of the guard to send twenty soldiers to Snake Island, who were to use any methods necessary to question Griselda on how she had breached the protection spell of the castle. Not having an alternative proposal, I watched the guards leave with a heavy conscience, taking comfort in the knowledge that it would take them weeks to arrive. If I found a solution before that, I could send a letter by owl post and rescue Griselda from her upcoming torture.

"Have you located the bespelled object that breached the castle's perimeter?" Father asked.

"No," replied the captain of the guard. "We didn't find any new object in the castle."

Father turned to Godmother. "Would you kindly search the palace for any magic?"

Godmother nodded. "I will. But if the guards haven't found anything, it could be that Griselda was just testing her power to see if she could reach the palace. After all, this was the first time that the alarm went off."

While my father talked more security-related issues over with the guards and Godmother, my gaze fell on a wooden figurine with a large head, wide grinning mouth, and cotton beard. The nutcracker had no place in Father's study. I stepped closer, recognizing the toy as the one Mother had bought for me before her death. It had been such a long time since I'd last seen it, I had believed it to be lost. I remembered searching for it for weeks, crying when I couldn't find it.

And now here it was, in Father's study of all places. Why had he kept it from me for all this time? Did he think it would be easier for me to get over the loss of my mother without having a reminder? Whatever his reasoning was, the temptation to hold something that provided even the tiniest connection to my mother was too strong to resist, and without asking, my hand closed around the painted red jacket. I brought the wooden boy up to my face to study him closer. A granite, sparkly vapor burst out of the nutcracker. My lungs inhaled the fumes, and my whole body contracted in excruciating pain, cramps racking me from head to toe. Still gripping the nutcracker, my knees gave out, and with a thump, I collapsed to the ground.

"What have you done, Clara?" Father screamed, but I couldn't reply as darkness blanketed me.

❦ 6 ❧

GRISELDA

"No! No!" I shrieked and tossed the mirror across the room, belatedly realizing I might destroy my magic weapon.

The mirror never hit the floor. Delilah caught it and strolled over to me, swinging her hips as she stepped over the sleeping bodies of our cellmates.

"What happened, Griselda? Didn't your plan work?" Delilah said with fake concern, pulling a curly, blonde strand of hair behind her ear.

A few bodies twitched on the floor, and few pairs of eyelids fluttered opened. Not wanting to wake anyone and draw attention to myself, I quickly said, "I'm fine. Just a nightmare."

Delilah gave me an I-don't-believe-you look. Unlike my unjust incarceration, she had been imprisoned for a reason. The Hamburg Police had discovered her kneeling above her bleeding father while her mother's broken form was in the gardens; she had been shoved off the balcony.

Delilah was dangerous, but I was willing to risk trusting her because I couldn't execute my escape plan alone.

I pulled Delilah deeper into the crevice I was sitting in and lowered my voice. "My magic set off an alarm in the castle. They know that I tried to attack them. They're sending guards to strap me down and torture me." I snatched the mirror out of Delilah's hands, wondering whether there was a point in eavesdropping more on the castle. No, I had no time. I needed to figure a way to escape before the Snake Island guards read the Austrian emperor's letter and strapped me down to hand me over to the Austrian guards. If Mother were here, she would give me a beating for not anticipating what had happened and for not preparing better. A dumb girl, that's what she would call me.

Delilah's voice snapped me back to the present. "That's a shame."

"You think so?" I let my sarcasm drip into the question, fantasizing about tearing out her perfect golden locks. Somehow, Delilah still managed to look like a noble in the prison. "That's not all. Clara's darn fairy godmother showed up, giving her advice. I was certain neither Clara nor the emperor could find the cure to the curse... but the godmother might just know it and provide suggestions on how to get it."

"A challenge. How exciting," Delilah singsonged.

My hand twitched to slap her across the face. Instead, I pulled each of my fingers hard, as if trying to rip them out of their sockets, forcing myself to be nice to Delilah since she was the only one who might aid me. "I need you to help me escape."

Delilah made a show of examining her hands, tracing the lines of her fingernails. "Why would I do that? Why should I help you and risk getting into trouble?"

I intertwined my fingers and pressed my palms together, the desire to slap her overwhelming now. "What do you want?" I hissed.

Her mouth split into a grin. "The mirror."

33

"I can't give you that. It's my mother's. It's the only thing I have of my mother's." My rage turned into something else, something much uglier—desperation.

Delilah tilted her head. "If you prefer to keep the mirror and be tortured, be my guest." She pivoted around, but I grabbed her wrist.

"Fine, I'll give you the mirror." Mother would be furious if she saw how easy I gave up and furious at the smug satisfaction on Delilah's face. What Delilah didn't know was that I had only agreed because I had realized I couldn't take the mirror with me. As a mouse, I couldn't carry such a large object, so I would have to return for it anyway. Delilah could use it until Clara succumbed to the curse and a hired assassin got rid of the emperor. Once I became empress, I would retrieve my mirror and wipe the smug expression off Delilah's face.

Delilah curled a blonde strand around her finger. "Now, what do you need me to do?"

I looked pointedly at her luscious curves that I knew none of the guards could resist. "Put that pretty body of yours to use. Pretend you're sick. I'm sure the guards will fall all over themselves to cater to your needs."

She tilted her head. "My acting is superb, but I'm afraid, they'll still notice you slipping out of the cell."

I smirked. Just thinking about shifting must have transformed my teeth, because Delilah's face paled. Strange how afraid most were of mice, such tiny creatures that couldn't inflict much damage compared to a lion or a wolf.

"Come on." I tried taking Delilah's arm, but she stepped away. Annoyance washed over me at her backtracking. "You'll be fine. They won't ever be able to prove that you were faking it. People get aches all the time that don't lead to anything. Just say it was premenstrual." Playing to her self-importance, I added, "Unless you're too chicken."

She rolled her eyes. "I'm not afraid." She took a few steps forward so that she was close to the door but not right in front of it and doubled over, coughing. "Argh." The pain-filled scream that tore out of her mouth was so real that if I weren't standing next to her, I would've been certain someone was ripping off her limbs. "This hurts so much," she wailed. "Help. Please, help me."

It took only a few minutes for the guards to rush toward the cell. I stayed in the shadows where no one noticed me and transformed. A tingle rushed through me, and my nose twitched. My ears pricked, and my intestines felt as if they turned inside out. I dropped to the ground, landing in a crouch, my clothes collapsing on top of me. A guard opened the door and rushed over to Delilah. Not giving them another glance and trying not to think about the loss of my mirror, I darted past them.

I was halfway down the corridor when a guard yelled, "One is missing. Damn it, the mouse shifter, Griselda, where is she?"

Maneuvering my way through a crack in the wall, I prayed there were no cats nearby. When no felines intercepted me and my paws hit the grass, I wanted to yelp with joy, until a guard screamed, "Release the gas!" I glanced up to find him standing on top of the building. Several cylinders were aimed at the ground and shot out a cloud of smoke.

The knockout gas encircled the perimeter, and I increased my tempo but was too slow. The air around me changed, taking on a bitter tang. My legs slowed, and my body begged me to rest. Only the image of me sitting on the gilded throne, Clara and the emperor dead, allowed me to push past the fatigue and run across the grass field surrounding the prison. Mother would be proud.

The Black Sea came into view, the waves exploded into foam as they reached the shore. I immersed myself into the salty water, washing off the sleeping gas that had seeped into my fur. As my mind slowly cleared, I threw one more glance at the prison that had stolen ten years of my life, then darted toward the ships.

Part one of my breakout plan was complete. Now, I needed to board a ship, one that wasn't full of cats, a common preventative measure against mice and rats. My ears tucked close to my head as an image of me being ripped open, a cat claw tearing out my guts, popped into my mind. Then I remembered Mother's words. *Fear is for weaklings. Don't be a weakling, Griselda.*

I ran faster. I refused to rot away as a mouse. I would find a ship and travel to Schönbrunn Palace to avenge my mother and seize the throne.

7

CLARA

I didn't know how much time had passed since I had collapsed on the ground, writhing in agony, but finally, the cramps released me. My vision was still blurry, and my throat opened and closed rapidly, eager to expel the food I had ingested earlier.

"Shh, it's over now." Father helped me to my feet and put me into a cushioned armchair.

"Take small sips." Godmother handed me a cup of tea with a zesty ginger aroma.

"What happened?" I glanced around the room, trying to remember what had caused the excruciating pain.

Father looked even angrier than he had before, his lips thin, his body radiating tension, but there was also something else on his face, something that I had only seen once before when I had been attacked by my stepmother—fear.

"Was I poisoned?"

"No," Godmother replied. "The foreign magic didn't breach the castle's protection but came through the letter portal, which somehow must've been widened to let through a nutcracker. The dark magic in the figurine was what trig-gered the alarm."

I blinked rapidly, not understanding what she was talking about. "But the nutcracker, it was mine. I had it as a child."

"Griselda must've taken it before she was imprisoned."

"How is that possible? I can't believe the guards didn't search her!" Father crossed his arms, and the guard by the door shrank back.

"It wasn't the guard's fault." Godmother gave a reassuring smile to the young guard. "Jacqueline must've given her daughter an invisible purse to store things away in. No one but the owner can see the bag."

At first, I wanted to protest, but then I remembered how when Griselda and I had played as children, my favorite toys would disappear inexplicably for several days and then myste-riously reappear. A flash of annoyance filled me. Why would she steal from me when I was willing to share with her? Because she couldn't help herself. She always needed more. There was always a bottomless sadness and emptiness about her that couldn't be filled. I swallowed hard, unsure what to do with the compassion that overcame me.

I looked to my left at the spot in the air that glowed with a faint blue light. All I knew about the portal was that a long time ago, a light magic user had created it, connecting our castle to other castles and the prison of Snake Island to allow an exchange of quick communications, a useful addition to owl post. "Is the portal repaired now?"

Godmother nodded. "Yes."

"I have already sent two letters through the portal, telling the Snake Island guards to isolate Griselda and watch her closely at all times. I haven't received a reply so far." Father clenched his jaw. "I've dispatched my guards, and as soon as they reach Snake Island, Griselda will pay for what she's done."

"What about the magic in the nutcracker?" I hesitated, afraid to ask my next question. "It didn't do any significant damage, right?" I was no longer in pain, and yet, a foreboding feeling swathed me, making the hairs on my arms stand up.

Godmother held up the nutcracker. "Griselda imbued this with a curse. Since it was yours and given to you by your mother, you had a special bond with the toy, allowing her to create a curse that was only evoked when you touched the nutcracker."

"What curse?" My eyes darted around the room for a mirror to check whether I had grown horns and a tail. I had a faint memory that after the cramps had started, an unfamiliar voice had spoken some words, but I had been in no state to pay attention to it.

"The curse—" Godmother began, but Father interrupted her.

"She doesn't need to hear about it." He patted my forehead. "Clara, there's no need to worry about this. I'll take care of it."

I tilted my head to look past him and at my godmother. "I still would like to know. Please."

Father sighed, and Godmother's eyes shone with sadness. "After you passed out, the nutcracker relayed that you have twelve days to break the curse. If you don't, your body will turn into a wooden figurine, and your soul will be trapped for all eternity inside the nutcracker."

Cold sweat broke out on my back as I realized how much worse the curse was than anything I had envisioned. I would have gladly taken a tail or become a shapeshifter. "How do I break it?"

"You won't be breaking it. The guards will," Father said.

"The magic nut Crackatook must be fed to the nutcracker."

"Crackatook," I repeated slowly. "I've never heard of it before. Where does it grow?"

Godmother gave me a sad smile. "It's a magical nut. It's not available in Vienna, and I do not know where it is. However, there's a village of magic users just outside your kingdom—Gumpoldskirchen. One of them should know where the Crackatook can be found."

"So, I have twelve days to find it or I will turn into a wooden figurine and my soul becomes trapped?"

Godmother nodded. "There's one more thing. If the nutcracker is taken to a magical land, its internal clock will speed up, meaning that what you believe to be only a few hours could constitute a whole lost day."

A shudder rushed through me. "How will I know how much time I have left?"

Godmother's throat worked. "With each passing day, the nutcracker will warn you about how many days remain."

A doll speaking was eerie, but I was glad there was a way to keep track of time passing.

"Don't worry about the Crackatook. The guards will take care of it." Father moved to the map that hung on his wall and rearranged some of the pins in our kingdom. "I have dispatched a team. They should arrive next morning at the village Gumpoldskirchen to question all magic users."

"What about the princes?"

Father raised an eyebrow at my question, probably thinking me strange for bringing this up when my life was in danger. While I was worried about turning into a wooden doll, I was still concerned about entering a marriage with the wrong person. "I think this could be a good task to see who truly cares about me. Make them search for the Crackatook." I didn't really believe any of them would find it, but the opportunity to escape the whole drama of courting was too tempting to give up.

Father clapped his hands together. "An excellent idea. The prince who finds Crackatook and breaks the curse shall become your husband."

"What?" How could my plan to get rid of the princes have backfired so badly?

"You said you wanted them to be tested, and there's no better test than someone rescuing your life. Whoever manages to do so, will prove that he is husband material."

Before I could come up with a counterargument, Father strode out of the study and instructed the messenger that the princes should assemble immediately in the ballroom.

"Don't you think it's a bit hasty to decide that whoever breaks the curse gets to be my husband?" I had to nearly run to keep up with Father's long strides.

"Not at all. Nothing is better proof that a prince is worthy of your hand in marriage than him saving your life. It is the ultimate test."

We reached the ballroom, which was empty but for the princes. I wondered whether my court was worried or had already dismissed the alarm going off and was continuing the celebrations somewhere else. No longer alone with Father, I didn't dare to argue with him. He might be lenient, but he wouldn't forgive me for challenging his authority in public.

Thus, I tried to reassure myself that giving this task to the princes meant Simon with his sweaty hands wouldn't get anywhere near me, and neither would Julian. He seemed like someone who excelled at book research but had no idea how to talk to people and would fail miserably in his efforts to convince the magic users to give him the location of the Crackatook.

This left Felix and Leon. I hoped the test would reveal whether Felix cared about other things besides money and if Leon was more than a pleasant companion. Perhaps Father was right after all, and it was a blessing that we could give this challenge to the princes.

"I have a task for you," Father began. "You must find the nut Crackatook and feed it to the nutcracker." He held up the wooden doll. "You have twelve days starting an hour ago. The prince who completes the task will marry Clara."

I bit my tongue, unsure how I felt about Father leaving out the reason behind the task. Sure, me being cursed could be used against our kingdom when it came to hashing out the details of an alliance, but lying to these men didn't seem right when I sensed in my gut that the task was much more dangerous than Father made it out to be.

The princes fell into a debate about the best way to secure the nut, how to travel to find magic folk, and if they should bring guards from their kingdom.

"No guards," I said. "You must complete this challenge on your own."

The princes glared in response to my condition. Father looked like he was about to protest my solitary search condition but then nodded, probably remembering that he had taught me from an early age that being a monarch was a lonely position, one which required making big decisions on your own and sacrificing your well-being for your subordinates.

Accepting my condition, the princes continued with their questions.

"Do we know what the nut looks like?" Julian asked, writing furiously in a notebook.

Felix crossed his arms. "Does a magical being protect the nut? How much is the nut worth? Is it made of gold?"

Simon bit his full lip. "Where will we stay on our journey?"

On and on it went. Were they going to debate for ten days and then search for two? That wouldn't do. I couldn't put my fate into their hands or that of my guards. I needed to take control, find a way to slip out of the castle. Since Father had insisted that the nutcracker stay in his study overnight, I would need to retrieve the figurine, take some coin, water, and food, and saddle Biscuit.

"Are you all right?" I jumped at the voice behind me, but relaxed as I realized it was Philip. On the one hand, I was happy that he remained in the castle where he was safe. On the other hand, for selfish reasons, I was disappointed that he hadn't been sent out to search for the Crackatook. I had seen Philip solve complicated riddles within minutes and was certain that his sharp mind would be a big help in the mission. Then again, he was one of the youngest guards and his suggestions would probably be dismissed by more experienced sentinels.

"I'm fine. Just tired." I manage a weak smile, which turned into a real one as Father announced the ending of the meeting. It would be a long night since I couldn't afford to sleep, but I was looking forward to getting out of my tight dress and redoing my hair in a style where hairpins didn't prick my scalp.

After the princes left, Father gave me a hug. "Go to bed, Clara. Get some sleep." He released me and turned to Philip, who was still behind me. "Escort her."

"Yes, Your Majesty."

Philip was uncharacteristically quiet on the walk to my chambers, but I didn't mind, preferring the silence. It was only when I reached out for the doorknob that Philip stopped me, closing his hand over mine.

"The emperor didn't tell us the whole story." It was more statement than a question. "What really happened, Clara? Why do you need the Crackatook?"

"It doesn't matter." Realizing how cold that sounded, I

added, "You don't have to worry about it. The princes or the sentries will get it."

He pivoted me by my shoulders so that I had to face him. "Please don't lie to me. I know you too well for you to get away with it, and... we're friends, aren't we? And friends don't lie."

I shook my head. "Trust me, you don't want to know."

"Yes, I do."

The determination in his voice told me he wouldn't let it go, so I motioned for him to come inside my chambers.

"The Crackatook is for me. I was cursed by a spell that was put into the nutcracker. If the Crackatook isn't fed to the nutcracker within twelve days, I'll...." I stopped, unable to continue.

"Then what?" Philip took my hands in his. "Tell me, Clara."

"I'll turn into wood, and my soul will be forever trapped in the nutcracker."

Philip squeezed his eyes shut and cursed, words that I had never heard him utter before rushing from his lips. When he opened his green eyes, they shone with intensity. "I won't let that happen. I'll find it."

Imagining Philip out there, endangering himself for something that was my fault, made my heart contract. I had been the one to touch the nutcracker; I should be the one to lift the curse and accept any danger that came with securing the Crackatook. "The emperor wants you here. He has the situation under control." Before Philip could protest, I turned away from him and began to take off my jewelry. "I'm very tired. I would like to rest now. It's been a long day."

"Of course," he said quickly, and my shoulders relaxed. Philip was too much of a gentleman to allow me to do something as uncouth as remove my jewelry in his presence. It was only when I heard the doorknob turn that I looked over my shoulder, trying to commit Philip's image to my mind. His tall, muscular body, his dark hair that always had a messy quality to it, his confident gait.

He glanced backward, and our gazes met and held for a long moment. I didn't know what he was thinking, but I wished I could tell him that he was my best friend and I would miss him dearly. But I couldn't. If I did, he would know I was planning something.

8

CLARA

To avoid drawing suspicion to myself by behaving unusually, I didn't send Iris away when she knocked on my chamber and insisted on helping me out of my corset and remove the pins from my hair. After she was done, I gave her a big hug, silently saying goodbye. "I hope you'll feel better, Iris."

"Please don't worry about me, Your Highness. I know you have a lot on your plate. This is a crucial time in your life." Iris's eyes shone with sadness, as if she sensed that much more was going on than foreign magic breaching the barrier and Father assigning an unusual task to my suitors.

We said goodnight, and I pulled on my sleeping gown and lay in bed for a good half an hour until the castle grew quiet. I slipped out of bed and put on my riding gear, a simple navy dress with buttons down the entire length of the front, which allowed me to ride easily, and leather boots. With my purple cloak on and the hood pulled low, I grabbed a gas lamp and tiptoed to my closet where I shoved my dresses out of the way to reveal the hidden door at the back. I opened it and hesitated. Was I really going to do this? Was it foolish of me to think that I could do anything to solve the curse? Would me trying only disappoint and scare Father? I bit my lip. Perhaps. But I couldn't just sit in my room like a coward. Taking a deep breath, I hurried down the narrow corridor toward Father's study. The tunnel was only wide enough for one person to go through at a time. It was dank, its walls slimy with mold. It had been built so that I could access the safest room in the castle quickly in case we were attacked. But tonight, I took the route to retrieve the nutcracker and begin my journey to find the Crackatook.

I reached the end of the tunnel and pressed my ear against the door, straining to hear any noise. Since only silence greeted me, I cautiously pressed down the door handle and entered the dark study.

The nutcracker had been placed in a sturdy glass cabinet with a big lock on it. "Dammit." How on earth was I supposed to break the lock?

A popping sound came from behind me, and I whipped around to find Godmother had appeared.

"What are you doing Clara?"

Caught red-handed, I had no choice but to speak the truth. "I came here for the nutcracker. I can't just let others save me while I stay in the castle, doing nothing." I wanted to say more, but Godmother held up her hand, silencing me.

"I agree. This is your quest. To find the Crackatook, you'll need help from the magic folk, and they don't help just anyone. I doubt they will help the princes, who are motivated by the promise of a rich kingdom and a beautiful bride. But your heart is pure, Clara. If anyone will be able to convince the magic folk to help them, it will be you." She pressed her fingertips to the lock, and it sprang open.

"Thank you." I took out the nutcracker and hid it inside my cloak.

"It would have been easy for you to sit back and let others

do the work, but you didn't. You have shown courage and determination, and I shall reward both." With these words, Godmother gave me a water skin and a loaf of bread.

I took them, even though I didn't understand why she was giving me something I could've easily obtained from the kitchen. "Thank you."

Godmother smiled. "You're a very kind girl, Clara. Most wouldn't have accepted my gift so graciously, presuming it to be too simple. Let me assure you that both items are far from simple. The water will never be empty, and the loaf of bread will never shrink, no matter how much of it you eat."

"Thank you, Godmother." I examined the gifts, awed at all the diverse properties of magic.

"One last thing." Godmother handed me a pouch big enough to put all the items I had inside. "This bag will be invisible to everyone besides you."

My chin went slack with shock. "Like Griselda's," I muttered.

Godmother opened the door leading to the corridor. "You should go now. The guards have just finished their patrol. You'll have ten minutes to leave the castle. Ride through the night to get a head start. As soon as the emperor realizes you're missing, he will send guards to retrieve you."

I hugged Godmother tightly. "Thank you for everything."

"Never stop being kind and brave, Clara. Those qualities will be rewarded."

With a heavy heart, I left the castle, saying goodbye to life as I knew it and my father. *Please don't be angry at my disobedience. Please forgive me, Father.*

The stables were quiet this time of the night, but Biscuit was wide awake and nuzzled her snout against my palm. I saddled her and led her out of the stables. It was a starry night, and the moon was almost full, providing enough light for me to ride confidently into the woods.

The deeper I went into the forest, the thicker the trees and underbrush grew, obscuring my path, but I pressed on, remembering Godmother's warning and fearing being dragged back to the castle.

To the left of me, the forest grew less dense, and Biscuit and I passed the first village. My relief at making it this far was short-lived when a bright torchlight blinded me, and two burly men with bows and arrows cut off my path.

"What do we have here?" one of them asked in a grating voice.

Biscuit threw her front legs up, neighing and buckling wildly. "Shh, it's going to be all right. Calm down, Biscuit." I tried to shove down the terror rising within me.

The men stepped closer.

"Let me through," I said, hoping they couldn't hear the quiver in my voice.

"I don't think so." They guffawed.

This wasn't good. Not good at all. My heart hammered in my chest, and panic threatened to overcome me. Knowing that standing still I was easy prey, I jerked the reins to the right and pressed my legs hard against Biscuit's sides, pushing her into a gallop. I had no idea who these men were or what they wanted, and I wasn't interested in finding out. An arrow whizzed an inch past my face, making a cry of terror escape from my throat. I tried to switch directions but was too slow. A second arrow embedded itself into Biscuit's side. She roared in pain and threw her head around wildly. My grasp on the reins slipped. I tried to hold on, but slid down the saddle, and then I was bucked off. With a dull thud, I landed on the hard earth, pain lancing up my spine and down my legs.

The two men were only steps away, advancing toward me and Biscuit. I pulled my hood lower. If they recognized me, everything would be over.

"How did you get the unicorn, girl? Did you steal it?"

Not replying, I reached for the dagger inside my cloak. I wasn't nearly as good as my guards, but at least I knew the basic moves. Still, I doubted I would be able to defeat two criminals.

The burly men came closer, their faces hard and worn, and I forced myself up to my feet, even though the pain in my ankle urged me to lie down.

"Answer us, girl." The bandit closest to me grabbed me roughly by the collar of my cloak, while the other walked over to Biscuit.

"Don't touch her!" I screamed and raised my dagger. Before I could jam it into the bandit's side, he twisted my wrist. A yelp left me as sharp pain traveled up my arm, and my blade cluttered to the ground.

"Don't make this harder on yourself than it has to be," he snarled.

"Get away from her. Now," a familiar voice sounded, and the bandit holding me turned to find his partner standing completely still with a blade against his throat. Philip. He had come for me.

Philip flashed his guard uniform. "I've already called for reinforcements, and the emperor will have you hung for this if you don't retreat immediately."

The guy holding me released me immediately and ran off into the woods. Philip gave a shove to the accomplice, and he too took off.

"Are you hurt?" Philip hurried over to me, his eyes searching me for wounds.

"No," I rubbed my aching wrist. "My wrist and ankle are slightly twisted, but they'll be fine." I hobbled over to Biscuit, who had been joined by Ace, Philip's horse. "We need to remove the arrow."

As I held Biscuit still, promising everything would be all right, Philip pulled out the arrow. Instead of blood gushing forward, there was just a small trickle, which soon stopped. I stared in awe at the rapidly closing wound. I knew Biscuit's unicorn blood was magical and allowed her to heal faster, but I had never realized how much faster. What other powers did she possess?

I was about to ask Philip but stopped when I noticed his hard stare.

"What were you thinking leaving in the middle of the night alone?" he asked.

"Did you really call for reinforcements?"

Philip pressed his lips together. "No, but I will if I have to. What were you doing?"

"You don't understand—"

"Oh, I think I understand very well. You are planning to retrieve the Crackatook yourself."

My forehead furrowed. "How did you know?"

He rolled his eyes. "Please, Clara, I've known you for most of my life. I knew you were planning something from the way you were acting when you said goodnight."

I lifted my chin, insulted and annoyed at him for being able to see through me so easily. "Thanks for helping me, but I need to get going now. And just so you know, this isn't a crazy plan. Godmother thinks it's the right thing to do as well."

"I didn't say that you should stay behind and do nothing. But you should have asked for help."

I laughed bitterly. "As if Father would've ever allowed me to venture out of the castle."

Philip grimaced and shook his head. "You should have asked me. I would have come with you."

I wanted to throw a witty remark at him, but didn't, noticing the hurt in his eyes. Instead, I whispered, "I didn't want to get you into trouble."

"Well, I'm here now. And I'm staying."

"Philip, no. This is my mission."

Not missing a beat, he replied, "You are the princess. As a royal guard, it's my duty to protect the royal family. And as a friend, it's my duty to protect you."

I bit my lip. "Philip, I don't want anything to happen to you. We don't know how long this journey might be and what we'll encounter, and I don't want you to lose your position when you return."

"I don't care about losing my position. If I lose you"—he tugged a hand through his hair—"I couldn't live with myself."

I sighed. Philip was just as stubborn as me. Standing around and arguing with him was a waste of time. I mounted Biscuit, and Philip mounted Ace and asked, "Now, where are we going?"

I smiled at Philip, grateful I didn't have to do this alone. "Gumpoldskirchen. The magic folk should know where the Crackatook is."

❧ 9 ❧

CLARA

We rode through the night and into dawn. The sun was rising on the horizon, bathing the lanky pine and fir trees in a soft, golden glow. Crisp air mixed with the scent of damp earth and apples. A sweet harp melody reached my ears. Even the most accomplished court musicians couldn't play as heavenly as this, making me certain that the harpist was a magic creature.

"We must be really close to Gumpoldskirchen."

Philip frowned, clearly not sharing my excitement. "We should rest and figure out a plan before we reach the village."

"But the princes and the guards—"

Philip rolled his eyes. "I've seen the princes. I doubt any of them rode through the night, and neither did the guards. It's not wise to exhaust the horses too much when one can't switch them at the destination. I'm certain we have enough of a head start on everyone. We can take twenty minutes to rest, eat, and go over strategy."

Begrudgingly, I followed him to a shallow river. Only when I got off my unicorn did I realize how much my back and thighs ached. My bones creaked as I stretched and sat on the ground, feeling like I could stay there forever. Biscuit and Ace drank from the creek, and Philip offered me a water skin, but I shook my head. "I have my own." I pulled it out. "God-mother said it will never become empty."

He gave it an appraising look. "Do you have magic apples and cheese too?"

"No, but I have bread." I shared it with Philip, Ace, and Biscuit, who were all mystified at how the bread regrew right in front of our eyes whenever I broke off a piece.

"I'm glad you came with me," I said, after a long silence.

"Me too. You know, you can be strong and let others help you. They're not exclusive." Philip stared into my eyes, giving me the feeling that he could read me like a book without me having to say anything.

I shook my head. "It's great to have somebody who has my back, but that's not what I meant. I'm glad you came because of your company."

He smiled, his gaze wandering briefly to my lips, and a strange fluttery feeling filled me. I realized we were so close that our arms were almost touching. Instead of moving away, I leaned forward. A rustling sounded behind me, shattering the moment, and I whipped my head around, relieved to see that it was just a small gray rabbit scurrying behind a bush.

Not wanting to think too much about what Philip and I had almost done, I rose and injected my voice with positivity. "Let's find the Crackatook."

Philip opened and closed his mouth, then mounted Ace and followed me and Biscuit. As we cantered closer to Gumpoldskirchen, the melodious music grew stronger and stronger until it seemed to be coming from everywhere. It wasn't painful or uncomfortable, just all-consuming. The music wasn't the only sign that alerted us that we were leaving the normal world behind. Around the perimeter of the village was a blue, glittering light. Even though it was beautiful, it made me shudder. Would it act like a barrier and keep us out? Or was it an alarm that would break loose when we crossed the threshold? Either way, we had to proceed cautiously, so Philip and I dismounted. We ended up walking next to each other, so close that we were almost touching. My skin tingled from the proximity, and yet I took comfort in his presence.

"I'll go first," Philip said.

Before I could reply, squawking broke the bespelling music. Half a dozen huge birds circled us from above, their heads and upper bodies that of an eagle, and their lower bodies that of a lion. Their predatory beaks and claws were rust colored, their bodies were tawny but for their head, chest, and wings that were a flint color. They were majestic, terrifying creatures.

"Griffins." My body froze with fear. The only magical animal I knew was Biscuit, who was inching backward with Ace. "It's all right," I said in a soothing voice. Biscuit and Ace stomped their hooves a few times before calming while I tried to figure out how to deal with the griffins circling us.

Philip reached for his bow, but I stopped him. "Don't. That will only make it worse."

I took a few steps closer, testing to see what the griffins would do. As I had expected, they descended from the sky, batting their huge wings. I forced myself to stand my ground and not inch backward.

"What are you doing here, humans?" A low voice emanated from the beak of the biggest creature, startling me. "You shouldn't be here. This is the magic folk's territory."

My instincts screamed at me to run and hide. Instead, I curtsied low, all the years of etiquette lessons finally paying off, and pressed down on Philip's back, signaling for him to bow.

"You are correct, these are not our lands," I began. "My name is Clara, Princess of Austria, and I have come here to seek the counsel of the magic folk. I have been cursed, and with no magic of my own, I kindly ask for their guidance."

The griffin tilted his head and nodded a second later. "She speaks the truth."

"She speaks the truth," the five griffins echoed behind him.

"You shall enter and get your answers," the leader said. "But as soon as you do, you must be on your way. If no one in the village knows the answers you seek, or if they don't want to give them to you, you must leave."

"I understand," I replied. The griffin gave Philip an expectant look, but Philip didn't make the promise, so I elbowed him.

"I understand," he said with a note of annoyance.

"Very well. You may pass."

The griffins took to the air again, and I carefully stepped into the blue light, breathing a sigh of relief when nothing zapped me or hurt me in any other manner.

"You shouldn't have agreed that quickly to their conditions," Philip grumbled.

I shot him an exasperated glare. "We don't have anything to bargain with. Plus, their conditions seemed fair to me." I tried not to think about what would happen if none of the inhabitants wanted to help me. From books, I had learned that the magic folk were volatile, their moods changing hourly.

I was temporarily distracted from my worries by the view opening in front of me. The most luscious grass and moss I'd ever seen surrounded me; in its center a cobblestone road had been laid. The trees were so tall that I couldn't see their tops, and huge mushrooms grew in a spiral fashion, creating odd-looking staircases. Each tree had several miniature doors and windows, and I caught a glimpse of tiny faces and wings inside—fairies.

There were also regular houses with colorful shutters and straw tops, which looked as soft as clouds. Thick vines grew from the earth and held up lamps, and straight ahead was a wide tree with several pots on its branches, which I presumed were houses as well. A rainbow as wide as a lake shone on the horizon, and in front of it was a skinny, red-rocked bridge, connecting two canyons.

Biscuit and Ace trotted toward it, as if they were certain that was where we would find our answers, but stopped sharp when a group of dwarfs with hammers and heavy bags slung across their shoulders marched across the path. The rust- and white-bearded males walked in a single row, not even giving us a passing glance. As with the griffins, I was awed to see beings that so far had only existed in my books. Shaking off my amazement, I forced my mouth to work. "Excuse me!"

None of the dwarfs reacted, so I jumped off Biscuit and fell into step with the males, surprised by how quick they could walk with their short legs. "Excuse me. Can you help me please?"

One of the dwarfs scowled at me. "Our jewels are not for sale."

"That's not why I'm here," I said quickly, having the distinct feeling that the helmeted men with their breast plates, shoulder guards, and metal gauntlets would be quick to pick a fight if they thought I wanted to steal their treasures. "I'm here to find the nut Crackatook. Have you ever heard of it?"

"Maybe once or twice." The dwarf's steps grew faster as he hurried to a cave the height of my waist with a wooden door where his group was disappearing into.

Doubting I would be allowed in, even if I could somehow squeeze through the tiny opening, I hurriedly said, "Please, if there's anything you know, tell me. I was cursed, and the only way to lift the curse is to obtain the Crackatook."

The dwarf paused in front of the wooden door and crossed his arms. "I've only heard it mentioned in a few stories. I don't know anything about it. Ask Daphne." Not telling me who Daphne was or where to find her, he slammed the door to the cave shut.

Philip made as if to open the door, but I stopped him. "Remember what we promised the griffin. The dwarf has given us enough of a pointer. We should go and find this Daphne."

I ambled through the village, wondering where all the inhabitants were. At work? Hiding in their homes? Did they know we were here and were avoiding us and our bothersome questions?

A splashing sounded behind me, and I pivoted around to find a pond, a scaled tail disappearing in the water. A second later, a face with long hair broke through the surface, and then a torso, naked but for the clam shells covering her chest. A mermaid. She was less beautiful and cheerful than my books described her. Her chin and nose were sharp and long, and she wore a bored expression.

"Excuse me, have you ever heard of the Crackatook?" I cut straight to the chase before the mermaid disappeared again.

She shook her head, her thick seaweed-colored hair sticking to her shoulders.

"Do you know who Daphne is and where we can find her?"

The mermaid grimaced and pointed with her head to a stocky tree with fuchsia pods on its branches. "Pixie," was the only word she said, then she dived.

"This feels like a wild goose chase." Philip took out his pocket watch. "We've been here for several hours without any results."

I took the watch from him. "That's impossible! We couldn't have been here longer than half an hour."

"We entered at nine and its twelve now. Time flows faster in magical realms."

"Oh, no." I reached for the inside pocket of my cloak and took out the white-bearded nutcracker dressed in his red-and-black soldier uniform. How much time did I have before he would announce that I had only eleven more days to break the curse? "We need to hurry up before we lose more time in this magical village." I sprinted to the tree, knocked against its rough bark, and screamed, "Daphne! Daphne!"

❧ 10 ❧

CLARA

A pixie with pink hair, the face of a twelve-year-old, orange wings, and a green dress flew out of one of the pods. "I might be small, but I'm not deaf." She lifted her button nose at us. "What do you want, humans?"

Not allowing her feistiness to intimidate me, I said, "I've been cursed, and I've come to seek guidance about where to find the nut Crackatook." At her blank look, I showed her the nutcracker. "The curse was in him and can only be broken when the nut is fed to him."

"And why would you think that I have the information you seek?"

"A dwarf told us to come to you." My shoulders dropped. Was I wasting my time? Had the dwarf told us to come to Daphne to get rid of us?

The pixie huffed, but then flew away from her house and hovered above the path. "Follow me. If anyone in this village knows where the Crackatook is, it's Mr. Drosselmeyer."

She fluttered her wings hard, and I had to mount Biscuit to keep up with her. "Who is this Mr...."

"Drosselmeyer. He's an inventor. He makes all kinds of things, fusing human inventions with our magic."

"And he's allowed to live in the magic village with you?"

She laughed, a tinkling sound. "More than allowed. We love having him here. He keeps us informed about what is going on outside and has saved us from a lot of trouble." She reached a straw-roofed house and knocked. "Mr. Drosselmeyer, I have someone who would like to see you."

"Let them in," a hoarse voice called.

The pixie flew away, Philip and I tied Biscuit and Ace outside the house then stepped through the door to find ourselves in a workroom with several long, wooden tables, shelves, and tools. Behind one of the tables stood a lanky man with an eyepatch, thick white hair, and a matching pointy beard.

"You came to see me? How can I help you?" he prompted.

I explained for what felt like the umpteenth time what had happened with the nutcracker. Once I was done, Mr. Drosselmeyer took the wooden doll from me, examining it. I held my breath. If he didn't have any answers for us, I didn't know what to do next.

"I'm happy to tell you the location of the nut Crackatook, but I'll require payment."

I exhaled. "Of course. I would be happy to pay in coin or jewels."

Mr. Drosselmeyer gave me a wry grin. "That won't do. I want the sword of the seven-headed Mouse King."

I blinked, thinking I must have misheard.

"There's a mouse with seven heads that is a king?" Philip asked.

"Correct. He lives in the Inverse Kingdom and protects the Crackatook." Mr. Drosselmeyer looked us both over. "It won't be easy for you to navigate the Inverse Kingdom. It is a deadly place."

I swallowed hard but refused to let my fear control me. "Where will this sword be?"

"On the Mouse King, and he'll also guard the Crackatook. Be careful. The Mouse King is known to fight dirty."

I rubbed my arms, trying to banish the shiver his words created. "Why do you want the sword?"

Mr. Drosselmeyer gave a close-lipped smile. "That is none of your concern."

All right. I supposed I didn't need to know. "Is this Mouse King related to my stepsister Griselda? She's a mouse shifter."

Mr. Drosselmeyer nodded. "The Mouse King was the one who brought mouse shifters into the human world before powerful fey magic banished him, forcing him to remain in the Inverse Kingdom. He'll know of your presence as soon as you enter his kingdom."

Before I could ask how, the grandfather clock hit 1:00 p.m., the nutcracker shook, and an eerie voice drifted from his mouth. "Only eleven more days remain. If you don't solve the curse, you'll turn into a wooden doll and your soul will be locked for all eternity inside of me."

If not for Philip's steady hand, I would've dropped the nutcracker. "It can't be." I fought the tears threatening to spill down my cheeks. "I should have at least six more hours until the first day is up."

Mr. Drosselmeyer pressed his lips into a firm line. "Time flows quicker here and is adversely affecting your curse. Let us go over the details of your journey and then you must be on your way."

My gut clenched. Was I really ready to do this? Disobeying Father and coming to Gumpoldskirchen to find the location of the Crackatook was one thing, going after it myself quite another.

Unaware of my thoughts, Mr. Drosselmeyer walked over to a light wood cabinet, opened a drawer, and pulled out a ball of golden yarn. "This will lead the way. As soon as you leave the village, simply hold on to the thread and throw the ball. It will roll its way straight to the entrance of each of the three magical kingdoms you must visit and finally the Inverse Kingdom."

"What?" I didn't have time to visit three magical kingdoms. "Can't we go straight to the Inverse Kingdom?"

Not replying, Mr. Drosselmeyer pressed the yarn ball into my palm. It fit easily, making me wonder how on earth it would be long enough to lead us to a different kingdom. I supposed magic didn't follow regular rules. It couldn't be dissected and analyzed.

"Each kingdom you pass will give you a challenge," Mr. Drosselmeyer said. "If you solve it, you will be rewarded. The gifts you receive will help you at the Inverse Kingdom. If you fail to collect them, you won't stand a chance."

"What kind of challenges and gifts?" I asked, thinking that cryptic should've been his middle name.

"That you'll have to find out for yourself." I wanted to protest, but Mr. Drosselmeyer held up his hand, silencing me. "What are you traveling by?"

"My unicorn, Biscuit, and Philip's horse, Ace."

"Very well. Your unicorn can use her horn to open the magic barriers separating our world and the magical dimensions."

Philip furrowed his forehead in confusion. "How will she do that? Do we need to help her?"

Mr. Drosselmeyer sighed. "No. You'll have to trust her. She'll instinctively know what to do."

I didn't like the sound of all this. Already this journey sounded much more perilous and complicated than anything I could've imagined. Father would be furious if he found out the danger I was exposing myself to. My heart ached as I realized that by now, he must've already noticed that I was gone.

Had Godmother told him what I was up to? Or was he going crazy with worry about my disappearance?

A bell chimed from outside, and Mr. Drosselmeyer stared at the door. "Looks like somebody else has reached our village."

I grabbed Philips hand. "The princes. Or the guards. We must leave now."

Mr. Drosselmeyer pushed the door open for us. "Good luck, and don't forget to collect my sword from the Mouse King."

"We won't," I reassured him, even though I was overwhelmed by all the information and everything we had to do.

Outside, we unbound Biscuit and Ace and made our way back to the fairy tree pods. Luckily, I spotted Daphne's pink hair and orange wings. "Daphne," I called.

She glanced back with an annoyed expression. "What do you want now?"

"Is there a second path out of the village? I'm afraid someone from my kingdom has arrived to take me back home."

She rolled her eyes. "Of course, you brought more humans to our place." She motioned with her hand. "Follow me."

She guided us back to the main entrance and pointed at a spot to the left. "This is the end of the entry. Whoever arrived is standing at the center where the griffins are. They might still see you, but you won't be in their direct line of vision."

"Thank you so much," I said, and Philip and I trotted out of the village through the blue light. Once we were on the other side, I heard the griffins arguing with a man.

"You don't understand, I need to get into this village," he said.

"I do understand, but your request has been denied," the griffin replied in a booming voice.

Overcome with curiosity, I glanced to my right to see who had reached the village first. The prince was medium built with a handsome face that was disfigured by a snarl. Felix.

"I'll fight you then." He drew his sword, and a gasp escaped me. His head whipped around, and his eyes locked with mine. "Clara. Clara!" The shock in his voice crystalized into ire.

I pressed my heels into Biscuit's sides and pushed her into a gallop.

"You shouldn't have stopped," Philip reprimanded, once we could no longer see Felix.

"I know. I just couldn't help myself. I needed to know who it was."

"Why? Do you like one of them?"

Did I? Maybe Leon. He had put me at ease, and he was funny and charming. But I didn't plan to admit this to Philip, so I stayed mum.

For a moment, it looked like Philip wouldn't let it go, but then he said, "We're far away from Felix now. Throw the ball of yarn, so that we can start our journey to the Inverse Kingdom."

GRISELDA

One wave after another crashed into the ship, rattling it. My stomach heaved, and bile rose up my esophagus. I tried to force back down the stolen bread and cheese I had inhaled this morning, but it was too late. A puree of biting acid filled my mouth, and I darted to the bucket in the corner, throwing up my breakfast.

Why is your body so weak, Griselda? Why can't you be more like me? Mother's words echoed in my head.

Wiping my mouth with the sleeve of my dress, I cursed. I wasn't weak. This was the water's fault. I had hoped my journey would get better once I had crossed the Black Sea and was traveling on the Danube River, but even the river proved too much for my motion sickness. I couldn't wait to reach Vienna, which unfortunately would take another four days.

My need to stay out of sight and undetected warred with my need for fresh air. I tried to stay as long as I could in the utility closet, but it was so small that I couldn't escape the rancid stink of my vomit. The bucket had to be emptied if I wanted my dry heaving to cease, at least for a while.

Cautiously, I pushed the door open and watched as a man wearing a white hat and carrying a tray of chicken soup disappeared behind a heavy, wooden door. My gag reflex returned and my stomach heaved. I breathed through it, reminding myself that soup being served meant lunch had just started and most of the sailors would go down to dine, giving me a higher chance of inhaling fresh air without being caught.

The rotten stairs creaked underneath me as I climbed my way up to the deck, wishing I could shift into my mouse form, which was so much easier to hide. Alas, I was in no shape to shift, and I couldn't carry the bucket in my tiny form. If I had to smell my vomit much longer, I swore I would be so violently sick, I might die.

I reached the bow, glad to discover my earlier assumption about lunch luring the crew away had been correct and that only two sailors monitored the ship. One was bulky with a wooden leg; the other was a lanky guy. They passed a bottle of rum between them, taking a long swig each time. I inhaled the fresh air, waiting for my stomach to settle and trying to ignore the sailors dimwitted conversation about the previous night's gambling.

How I wished I still had my magic mirror and could check up on Clara, see what she was up to. Was Delilah using it now to spy on her brother who had put her in prison? I shivered as I considered what she would do to him if she ever escaped the prison. I wanted Clara and the emperor dead and out of my way, but Delilah wouldn't be satisfied with that. She would torture her brother, drive him to insanity. Best not to think about what she would do to him.

With my gag reflex calmed, I turned to leave, only to stop in my tracks as the bulky guy with the wooden leg said, "The captain received the oddest owl post today."

"What's that?" his tall companion asked.

"Well, apparently, Princess Clara of Austria has gone

missing after her coming-of-age ball. The emperor gave her suitors a silly task to find a nut." He shrugged, as if to say that royals were eccentric idiots. "But on the next day, when the princes were supposed to start the task, the princess—" He paused dramatically, his eyes bulging out with excitement. "—disappeared."

"You think she's afraid of the wedding night?"

As both men guffawed, my hands shook with rage, and I cursed Delilah. Then I cursed my mother, who hadn't taught me how to shrink the mirror when I needed it to be smaller for my mouse form. I knew such magic existed, and if I had owned it, I wouldn't have needed to leave the mirror behind at Snake Island and rely on getting my information from two drunk sailors.

Knowing that dwelling on what I didn't have would get me nowhere, I tried to think about the situation in a rational way. Perhaps my meticulous plan wasn't in danger. So what if Clara had left? That didn't mean she would discover the Crackatook.

Or did it? On several occasions, I had observed Clara through the mirror as she argued her way out of situations she didn't like.

My eyelid twitched. I had underestimated Clara's willpower. I couldn't afford to underestimate her ability to succeed in finding the Crackatook. After all, her mother, who had possessed what was deemed as light or holy magic, had left a unicorn to Clara.

My stomach tightened into rigid knots. I had banked on no one getting as far as finding the place where the Crackatook was hidden. But the magic village Gumpoldskirchen was known in Vienna. Clara with her annoyingly friendly personality might cajole the magic folk into revealing the location of the Crackatook, and her unicorn would allow her to enter magical dimensions, such as the Inverse Kingdom.

I set the metal bucket down, no longer concerned with emptying it or putting it back in the correct place, and focused on the endless water in front of me. Four more days until we reached Vienna. Another day until I reached the Inverse Kingdom. As a mouse shifter, I could enter my homeland through several portals, not just the main entry that would be available to Clara and her unicorn, but even so, I had to find a portal first.

What if Clara was faster than me? What if she managed to sneak into the Inverse Kingdom before me? I needed to warn the Mouse King that she was coming. If he were to expect her, he could pull out all the stops and ensure she died before she stole the Crackatook—and he would pull out all the stops. After all, an ancient prophecy foretold that a young girl, aged seventeen, would bring down our king. The Mouse King wouldn't take the risk of Clara becoming that girl.

Yes, the king was my solution to the problem. I needed to reach the Inverse Kingdom and inform him that Clara was on her way. After I helped him get rid of her, his gratefulness would put me on the Austrian throne.

❧ 12 ❧

CLARA

The ball of yarn rolled for what felt like forever, and we followed it, galloping through the thick pine and fir forest. Just when I reached the point of exhaustion, certain I was about to fall off Biscuit, the ball rolled to a stop and a blue light shimmered into view. Biscuit tapped her horn against it, making a blue archway appear. I blinked repeatedly, but the portal remained. One moment we were surrounded only by forest, the next a passage had manifested out of thin air.

"This must be the first magical kingdom," Philip said slowly, his forehead wrinkling with concern.

"Yes." I swallowed hard, worried where the portal led to. It looked as if I would simply be stepping through to the other side of the forest, but of course I wouldn't. Once I entered the archway, there was no going back. Then again, there had been no going back ever since I had touched the nutcracker and unleashed the curse. My carelessness had brought me here, and now, it was up to me to set things right. I owed it to Father. I couldn't put him through more pain and loss. "Ready?" Philip asked, his voice tense.

"Let's do this on three." I held on tightly to Biscuit's reins. "One. Two—" A twig snapped behind me, alerting me that we weren't alone. I whirled around to find a tall, grim-faced horseback rider trotting calmly toward us. A golden crown with sapphires adorned his head, matching his blue-and-gold cloak.

"Julian," I gasped as soon as I regained my ability to speak.

He gave a half nod. "I knew Felix's choice to confront you at Gumpoldskirchen was a poor one. It's much better to talk when we aren't surrounded by griffins, don't you agree?"

I didn't appreciate his haughty tone but chose to ignore it. "How did you find us?" It was impossible for him to follow us for several hours without us spotting him... unless, he had magic of his own. I exchanged a glance with Philip, whose widened eyes told me he had come to the same conclusion.

Julian extended his hand. "Come back with me to Vienna, Clara. You'll be safe there. We'll solve the riddle of the Crack-atook together."

"I can't. You don't understand."

He tilted his head. "Oh, but I do. You want to decide who to marry and not be at the mercy of the task. Don't worry, I can assure you that I will be the best choice." He was an arm's length away now, and I was certain that if I allowed this conversation to continue, he would find a way to take me back to Vienna. I couldn't let that happen, so I had to face my fear of magic. "One," I said and jumped into the portal.

A strong wind seized me, twirling around, making me feel like I was in the heart of a tornado. Everything spun so quickly, I had no idea where left and right was or up and down, and there was a stabbing ache in my head. Just as abruptly as the uncomfortable sensation had begun, it ceased. The first thing I saw were Philip's green eyes. I exhaled, relieved that we hadn't been separated.

Philip gave me a lopsided grin. "Looks like Julian isn't your front runner."

I hit him on the shoulder as a gust of wind smashed into me from behind and then something big and heavy toppled into my back, making Biscuit jump forward and nearly bucking me off. I turned around to find Julian.

"Julian! You followed us!"

"Of course. Did you expect me to let you go off with him?" Julian glared at Philip.

"If you're going to be stubborn and insist on finding the Crackatook, I'm coming with you."

I rolled my eyes at him. "I'm not stubborn. I need to do this." After a beat, I added, "This will be dangerous. This is not one of your books that you can study, develop a theory, then prove or disprove it. This is real life." As if to underline my statement, a high-pitched howl tore through the air.

For the first time since stepping through the archway, I took in my new surroundings. Gone were the tall trees and the lush forest grass. In its place were rocks and tumbleweeds rolling in the arid wind. The air was no longer moist, but straw dry, and the temperature was at least ten degrees higher. I had only ever seen this climate described in geography books, and what I had read about it didn't make it seem like a pleasant one. "We're in the desert," I whispered, dismounting Biscuit.

"That's impossible! It must be an illusion." Julian shoved his way past me and touched a cactus, only to jerk his hand back and stare at the blood flowing from his pricked finger.

"Still think this is an illusion?" I asked, trying to hide my smile.

"A real desert? A real desert! How can this be?" He kept muttering to himself.

I drowned him out, focusing on Philip. "I sure am happy my godmother gave me the refillable water skin and the never-ending loaf of bread. I doubt we'll be able to find food or water here."

Philip glanced around. "I'm more concerned about turning into food."

I winced as a howling rang through the air. The desert was home to the coyote, and I sure didn't want to meet a wild canine, let alone a whole pack, if they traveled by pack. Something pushed against my foot. At first, I thought it was Julian stepping on my toes. The rattling noise and tightening sensation made me look down and gasp. A snake was winding itself around my ankle—and not just any snake. The wide head, keeled rough scales, and rattle on the tail identified it as a rattlesnake. I let out a piercing shriek and practically threw myself into Philip's arms. He pulled his sword and embedded it into the reptile, cutting it in half.

My breath came in quick gasps as I stared at the now dead snake. "Thank you."

"So that's why you're so disinterested and cold." Julian scowled and crossed his arms.

I straightened my spine, not wanting to show weakness in front of him, and calmly said, "I don't know what you mean."

"You're into the help." Julian smirked. "Plenty of regents keep someone on the side, even though it is more common for men than women. While it's disgusting, they have at least the taste and decency to choose someone from court. But the help, really? Do you have no self-respect whatsoever?"

Philip's chest puffed out. "We're friends," he said tightly.

After everything I had been through in the last two hours, I didn't possess as much self-restraint as he did. I slapped Julian's cheek hard. "Do not ever talk about me like you know me. You know nothing about me. And do not ever call Philip the help again. He's a respected member of the Guard and an honest person."

Rage danced on Julian's face. "What would your father say

if he knew you assaulted a prince to protect your precious help?"

Clenching my jaw, I didn't reply anything, not wanting Julian to know how much his words hurt me. I had slapped him, but he was poking my heart.

"I'd be careful if I were be you," Julian continued. "Austria is prosperous, but neither you nor your father are good at strategy or long-term planning. You'll run your kingdom into the ground, and when you do, I'll attack."

I gave him a hard smile. "Good to know what you really think."

He stiffened, probably realizing that he had not only lost my hand in marriage but any chance at an alliance. "How do I get out of here? Where did the archway go?"

"We need to complete our task, and then Biscuit will lead us out of here." I didn't mention that I had no idea what the task was or how we would find an archway. The archway into this desert realm had appeared out of thin air, but I worried that finding an exit wouldn't be as easy.

"Great, so until then I'm trapped with you." Julian threw us a dirty glare, as if he hadn't followed us willingly into the desert.

We hiked for ages without seeing any houses or people, just cacti, a few lizards, and hares. The sun beat down on our napes, slowing our trek. While I was tempted to ditch Julian after everything he had said, I couldn't bring myself to do so. Thus, I shared my waterskin and loaf of bread with him, hoping he was too grateful to attempt to steal the gifts my godmother had given me.

When the sun began to set and the temperature dropped, a clock chimed. Had I become delusional from exhaustion and imagined the sound? There were no clocks in the middle of the desert, yet I heard it clear and loud in my ears, and then the dreadful eerie voice drifted out of the nutcracker's mouth. "Only ten more days remain. If you don't solve the curse, you'll turn into a wooden doll and your soul will be locked for all eternity inside of me." I took out the nutcracker from my invisible purse, wishing I could smash it into pieces and be done with it. Why had I been stupid enough to pick up a toy I hadn't seen in ten years? How couldn't I have sensed that something was wrong with it?

"What the...? Did the doll just speak?" Julian tried taking the nutcracker from me, but I hid it. "Let me see!"

"It's not yours. Leave her alone." Philip shielded me, and even though I was grateful for his support, I hated dragging him into this. Because while Julian had only threatened me so far, I was certain he wasn't above doing something to Philip for the perceived rudeness he had to endure today.

We continued our trek, and Julian stayed quiet for a few minutes before exclaiming, "That's why you're set on getting the Crackatook. You'll die if you don't find it."

I pressed my lips together at the glee in his eyes. My reaction only spurred him on, and he chuckled. "You've been cursed. This whole time I thought it was us, the princes, fighting for you. But it's you who is at our mercy."

Philip, who had been clenching his fists for the last few minutes, grabbed Julian by his collar. "Shut up, or I swear I will tie you up and leave you out here to die. Clara might be too good of a person to let you rot in this desert, but I'm not."

Julian's eyes widened in fear, and his throat bobbed up and down.

"Do you understand me?"

Julian nodded weakly and stuttered, "Yes, I do."

"Good." Philip let go of Julian, who toppled backward, and focused on me. "Whatever we're meant to do here, I don't think it has to do with people. We've been searching the whole day and haven't found any. I think our answer lies with the animals. We need to seek them out instead of avoiding them."

I swallowed hard. Even after dealing with dwarfs, pixies, and griffins, the idea of approaching wild animals terrified me. I had heard that some of them had the ability to speak, but that didn't mean they had lost their feral qualities. However, Philip was right. Searching for people or houses had brought us nowhere, and we were running out of time.

"I guess we're lucky that desert animals tend to come out at night." I licked my lips nervously. "Shouldn't be too hard to find them."

Julian, who had stayed quiet since Philip's threat, pointed at a cave. "If you want to find animals, you should check in there. I'll sit this one out. I'm not interested in getting ripped to shreds by a wild beast."

"Fine by me," I replied, relieved since Julian would only be a distraction. Knowing the cave was too low for Biscuit and Ace to enter, I tied their reins around a gangly sapling with tiny, lime-colored leaves. I was certain Biscuit could pull it out with its roots if she wanted to, yet with no other option in sight, I decided it was better than nothing.

"I'll take care of Julian," Philip whispered. Before I could ask what that meant, Philip shoved Julian to the ground and tied his arms behind his back.

"What are you doing? You can't do that! I'm a prince! You'll be hung for this!" The vein in Julian's forehead throbbed so wildly, I was worried it might burst. Philip ignored Julian's rant and bound his torso to a tree opposite from where Biscuit and Ace stood. Satisfied with his handi-work, Philip gave me a smile. "Ready when you are."

I couldn't suppress my smile at Julian twisting against the tree, trying to get free to no avail. However, as we walked away from him, I felt a pang in my chest for leaving him tied up at the mercy of any passing animals. Then I reminded myself of all the nasty things he had said to me and that he would probably steal Biscuit and Ace if we didn't restrain him, and my guilt melted away.

Philip and I took our time, treading carefully toward the cave on the uneven ground compromised of different sized rocks and pebbles, the waning moon illuminating only parts of the landscape around us. A hiss made me freeze. A red snake with white and black stripes slithered toward us. Not knowing whether it was harmless or venomous, my shoulders only relaxed when it ignored us and went a different direction. Even though everything inside of me screamed to leave and run back, I pressed on, telling myself a snakebite was preferable to turning to wood.

When we reached the cave's entrance, Philip lit a match. We shuffled down the uneven, slick stone surface, keeping an eye on our horses until the path swerved sharply to the left.

"I'll go," I said. "You should keep an eye on the horses and Julian."

Philip shook his head and took my hand. "They'll be fine. I'm coming with you."

His warm, slightly calloused hand felt good in mine, and my intention to insist that he stay behind evaporated. Philip was right—Julian and the horse would be fine, but I needed him.

Holding hands, we took the left turn where the cave grew narrower and lower. Sharp edges jutted out from the cave walls, pressing hard into my shoulders and snagging my clothes. It was darker in here, and I could no longer see Biscuit, Ace, or the path out of the cave. Something scurried past my feet, making my skin crawl. The cave seemed to shrink in on me, and I found it hard to breathe, my chest constricting. We were too deep in, I couldn't stand being in such a tight space. I needed to get out. No, I couldn't. I needed to prevail.

I forced myself to take another step, but instead of meeting hard stone, my sole connected with something soft and rustling, like a mound of leaves, and plunged through the ground. A yelp tore out of me, and I tried to lean back to maintain my footing, but a howling wind shoved hard against my back, pushing me and Philip into the hole. I grasped for something, anything to hold on to, but my hands only met the smooth cave's ground. Unable to find purchase, I tumbled through the dusty air into the abyss, my last thought being, *I'm sorry, Father. I tried my best.*

13

CLARA

As I fell into the pit, I screamed my lungs out and flailed my arms, hoping to grasp on to something but only met air that didn't slow my descent. Philip grabbed my hand and managed somehow to position himself underneath me as we continued to fall.

"What are you doing?" I shrieked, my voice echoing.

"Making sure you don't get hurt."

"No." I tried to push him away. "I'll crush you."

"I don't care."

I wanted to protest more, but at this point I noticed that the blackness below us had changed to a lighter color. Was this the end? Too taken aback by our impending death, I shut up and squeezed my eyes closed. My last act in life was that of a coward, but I couldn't help myself, heights had always inspired terror within me.

The air was knocked out of my belly as I fell on top of Philip, praying I hadn't broken his spine. A bouncing sensation went through me, pushing me upward. Was that what death felt like?

I didn't dare to move out of fear of making this worse, and

it was only when Philip's fingers trailed down my cheek and he whispered, "We're fine," repeatedly that I dared to open my eyes.

He nudged me off him, and my body tingled in all the places it had been pressed against his. Heat filled me until I realized we were lying on a spiderweb. The icky, sticky, and surprisingly thick substance had saved our lives. I wanted to be grateful, but my skin crawled as I imagined how many spiders it took to build such a sturdy net.

Philip's usually bronze skin was chalky. However, unlike me, he wasn't frozen by shock. He pressed his face close to the net. "We're only a few feet away from the ground. Let's get out of here." He produced a knife from his pocket and cut a hole into the spiderweb.

The net collapsed, and I landed awkwardly on the cave floor, the impact reverberating through my spine. I pulled off the sticky spiderwebs that clung to my clothes and skin while praying that no huge spider was waiting for us. Out of the corner of my eye, I did notice a few spiders scuttering across the ground. Thankfully, they weren't too big and ignored us. The same couldn't be said for a tawny-colored scorpion the size of my forearm perched on a pedestal-looking rock.

"I hope you brought me gifts for disturbing me," he said in a whisky-smooth voice.

I stared at him, lost for words. Although I had prepared myself for animals to speak in the magical kingdoms, a scorpion doing so was still too much for me to handle.

Out of his pocket Philip pulled a pouch and presented it with a low bow to the scorpion, who clicked his fingers—or claws, whatever they were called—together.

"Worms, hmm, I suppose that will do." He devoured the worms in a few bites, and I shot Philip a curious and grateful glance.

"You never know what might come in handy. I planned to

use those suckers to catch fish." He shrugged nonchalantly, as if his quick thinking wasn't a big deal.

Done with his food, the scorpion crawled to the edge of his rock, and I had to restrain myself from stepping back. Could scorpions jump? How far? What if he jumped straight for my neck and bit me? Wait, wasn't its poison located in its tail?

Philip elbowed me, and I realized the scorpion had asked me something and was now awaiting a reply.

"Probably best if Clara tells you her story from the start," Philip said, throwing me a lifeline.

"Right. Of course." I hurried through my tale, beginning with my stepsister shifting into a mouse, her banishment, her magic sneaking into the castle, me touching the nutcracker, and unleashing the curse. "The only way to break the curse is to find the Crackatook and feed it to the nutcracker," I finished.

The scorpion tilted his head. "Very well. Since you've brought me a gift, I'm feeling generous, and I will make this easy for you." The malice emanating from him contradicted his words. "If you solve my riddle, I will give you my poison, which is the gift of paralyzation. However, if you fail to solve my riddle, you will become personally acquainted with my poison."

There was a rustling, and with horror, I discovered the scorpion we were talking to wasn't the only one in the cave. Onyx-colored scorpions the size of my hand emerged from all directions, clattering as they hurried toward us on their eight legs. There were at least one hundred of them, and their eyes shone with hunger while their tails undulated with menace. My chest contracted as I imagined being paralyzed with their venom, then coated in digestive juices that would break down my body to aid the digestion of the horrendous creatures.

"Do you accept my offer?"

I hesitated, certain the scorpion's gift would come in handy at the Inverse Kingdom but nervous that we wouldn't solve the riddle and end up as arachnid food. A chime sounded, and this time, I knew it was coming from my bag. The nutcracker shifted, and then his eerie voice spoke the words I dreaded most. "Only nine more days remain. If you don't solve the curse, you'll turn into a wooden doll and your soul will be locked for all eternity inside of me."

I refused to be trapped inside a doll. I refused to stay alive without being able to live. A quick and painful death was preferable to a life of misery. I knew Father wouldn't see it that way. He would argue that as long as I was in the nutcracker, there was still hope that someone might break the spell one day. Me risking immediate death would be wrong in his eyes. But this wasn't about his life, it was about mine, and I deserved to decide what to do with it and what risks to take.

My spine hardened, and I stared down the scorpion. "How many guesses do we get?"

The scorpion scrambled up and down, the clicking of his pincers echoing in the cave. "Three in total. I don't care who provides the answer, as long as we're clear that you will both be injected with my venom if you fail."

I turned to Philip to argue that I would do this task alone, so that only I had to bear the consequences, but he shook his head vehemently. "We're doing this together."

The scorpion swung his long tail, giving us a good view of his hairy, bulbous stinger and making my skin crawl. "So, are you in? You only have ten minutes to solve the riddle and time starts now."

"We're in," we replied in unison, and more rustling sounded as the scorpions crawled closer, some stopping less than an inch away from my feet.

The top scorpion cleared his throat and said in a loud

voice, "I can start a war or end one, I can give you the strength of heroes or leave you powerless, I might be snared with a glance, but no force can compel me to stay. What am I?"

My throat went dry. I had no idea. Could this answer be in one of the many books Father had recommended I read, and I had forsaken for an afternoon in nature? I strained my mind. There had to be something that fit the description of the riddle. "Confidence." The word slipped off my tongue, and I bit my lip, realizing I should've consulted Philip, not blurted out the first answer that came to me.

The scorpion snickered with delight. "Wrong answer. Two more tries."

Philip tugged on my sleeve, and I faced him. "Let's not hurry. We have ten minutes to discuss this before we make any more guesses."

I glanced at the scorpion, not wanting to risk his wrath. "Is it all right if we talk to each other?"

"Sure, but you only have ten minutes to solve the riddle, and one minute has already passed."

"What else can start and end a war?" Philip looked at me expectantly.

"Lots of things," I replied. "But they're all opposites. Greed, jealousy, envy, hurt, and pride can all start a war. Strategy, compromise, and reason could end one."

"Maybe we should move on to the next part: I can give you the strength of heroes or leave you powerless."

"Magic?" I ventured. "And it could both start and end war."

"But does it fit the last part: I might be snared with a glance, but no force can compel me to stay?"

I considered this for a moment. "Well, I suppose magic often has power over the compeller, and it's unpredictable, so it sort of makes sense. It doesn't fit perfectly, but—"

"Five minutes left," the scorpion interrupted.

Why was time passing so quickly? "Are you okay with me giving magic as the second answer?"

Philip nodded but looked concerned. "I guess. I can't think of anything better, so we might as well try."

"Magic." I held my breath as I waited for the scorpion's reply.

"Wrong! One more try left and four and a half minutes remaining."

I wanted to curse him. How did he even know the time? And why was I always giving the wrong answer? Why did I never respond how Bernadette and Father wanted me to? Was this going to be the punishment for my restlessness—death due to lack of knowledge?

"We need to focus." Philip squeezed my hand and reassuring warmth traveled up my arm. "We're looking for something that can start and end wars, give strength or leave one powerless, something unpredictable that comes and goes as it pleases."

I pulled on a loose thread on my dress. "That doesn't make any sense. I can think of a few answers that sort of fit, but none are a perfect match."

"Let's think back to wars described in history books and what started them."

I racked my brain and came up with more incidents of jealousy, hurt pride, and anger. While all of them could sort of fit the mold, I doubted that either of them was the correct answer.

Philip straightened, his eyes glinting with hope. "The Trojan War."

"Only one more minute to go," the scorpion hissed.

"It was started because of Helena and Aphrodite."

I wrinkled my forehead. "Are you saying women or pretty

women are the solution?" While I could sort of see it, I thought it was incredibly misogynistic.

"Ten. Nine. Eight," the scorpion counted down.

Philip's Adam's apple moved up and down. "Do you trust me?"

"Yes." I didn't even have to think about it. I trusted Philip implicitly with everything, including my life. He was my best friend. "Give him the answer you believe is right." I squeezed Philip's hand hard, crushing it, putting all my hope into him.

"Three. Two," the scorpion continued.

"Love," Philip said.

🎄 14 🎄

CLARA

The scorpion and Philip locked gazes and remained in a stare down for several seconds. I didn't dare to move, unsure what the silence meant. Had we just lost or won?

"Correct. You have proven teamwork and smarts. I will give you the gift of paralyzation, which will aid you at the Inverse Palace. But your journey is far from over. You will be tested many more times, starting by figuring out how to get out of the desert."

At that moment, I couldn't have cared less about future challenges. We had passed the test! No scorpions would eat us alive, and we were about to collect our first gift, which according to Mr. Drosselmeyer would help us retrieve the Crackatook from the Mouse King.

While I was hugging Philip, muttering, "I can't believe it. You got it right," the scorpion disappeared only to reappear with a tiny, white vial. I stored it away in my invisible purse, afraid he might change his mind.

"How do we get out of here?" Philip asked, staring up at the hole we hadn't seen earlier and had fallen through.

"That's for you to figure out." With that the scorpion vanished into the darkness of the lower cave, and so did his small brothers and sisters in a loud rustling, which was followed by a deadly quiet.

"Do you still remember how to climb?" Philip asked.

I gave him a smile, grateful that my childhood tree-climbing escapades were finally paying off. "Yes." I put my foot on the uneven cave wall and pulled myself up. My upper body strength was lacking, but my legs were strong and flexible, allowing me to successfully ascend. "I wish we would have been more careful and avoided falling into the trap." I reached higher, making my way slowly up.

"Yes, but then we wouldn't have collected the gift of paralyzation. Everything works out the way it's meant to be," Philip said from behind me.

"How wise of you." I continued my climb, grateful that Philip was behind me, in case I slipped. My gratefulness turned to dread when I reached a patch of thick spiderwebs with several furry spiders.

Philip must've noticed my hesitation, because he asked, "Do you want me to clear it for you?"

"No, I'm fine." I swallowed my disgust and put my hands into the sticky cobwebs, reminding myself that as disgusting as this was, it had saved our lives less than an hour ago. Plus, if I was afraid of getting dirty, I should've stayed at the palace and placed my fate into the hands of the princes and the guards. But I hadn't, and I was glad I was here, fighting for myself. I only wished that I could've made this choice with Father's approval and without worrying and disappointing him.

While my feet slipped a few times, I never lost my footing completely. Finally, I reached the upper part of the cave and pulled myself up. I lay on my back, breathing hard. My heart wanted to hurry to Biscuit and Ace, but my body demanded a break. Philip and I caught our breath, and I checked that the nutcracker was still safely tugged away inside my invisible purse, which I had stuck into the large inner pocket of my cloak.

We exited the cave, and I froze at the sight of the lonely trees. Biscuit, Ace, and Julian were gone.

"Dammit," Philip cursed next to me, examining the yellow-greenish saplings he had bound the horses to. "Julian got out of his bindings."

"What do we do?" I asked.

Philip put his fingers into his mouth and whistled loudly, and I followed suit, hoping either Biscuit or Ace would hear us and come dashing. Our efforts were in vain.

"How do we find them?" Desperation rose to the surface, ready to consume me.

Philip thought about this for a moment. "Julian wants the same thing as us, to get out of this place. The archway we came through vanished. He's probably trying to find the exit."

I nodded, wondering where t the portal could be. "Maybe this will help us." I pulled out the golden yarn of wool and threw it onto the ground, hoping it would show us the way. It rolled about a foot to the left but then stopped. "Come on, come on," I encouraged it.

"It already gave us all we need to know. We need to go northeast." Philip pointed to the left, and we hurried that way as fast as we could without tripping on the uneven ground.

We ran for what felt like forever. I pressed on even when my knees cracked, my shins ached, and a side stitch built below my left ribs. Philip better be right about this being the correct direction, because if it wasn't, I doubted I could even crawl back. Eventually, we were both out of breath and our legs gave out, forcing us to pause. I took out the water skin, and we emptied it fully, and its next two refills as well as sharing probably a loaf of bread—hard to tell when it kept regrowing as soon as we broke off a piece.

"Did you hear that?" Philip asked, and I strained my ears to recognize the sweetest sound—a quiet neigh. I ran toward it and stopped behind a copse of fine-bodied trees, Biscuit and Ace less than ten feet away from me. Julian's hand was on Biscuit's bridle, and he was jerking it none too gently to make her hit her horn against a blue light emanating from the center of a red-rocked mountain. I started off toward him, but Philip pulled me back. Unsheathing his sword, he said, "If you don't mind, I would really like to handle this nitwit."

I gave him a wide, genuine smile. "Please, be my guest."

Philip sneaked up on Julian just as Ace turned, noticing his owner. I was afraid he would give Philip away, but he didn't make any noise, as if knowing he needed to remain quiet.

Philip knocked the pommel of his sword hard against the back of Julian's head. Julian swayed and collapsed. Before he could hit the ground, Philip grabbed him underneath his armpits and lifted him up and onto Ace, using Julian's belt to secure him to the saddle.

"My work is done." Philip motioned to the rock. "Now it's your turn to convince Biscuit that we need to get out of this desert before somebody makes us dinner." A coyote howled, underlining Philip's words.

I petted Biscuit and brushed my fingers through her mane. "I need you to get us out of here. I need you to open the portal." I hugged her. "Please, Biscuit, try it for me."

She neighed gently, and then she focused her attention on the blue light emanating from the red rock wall in front of her. A gentle tap of her horn against the surface didn't do anything. She tried different points, creating a rapid knock-knock pattern without any results.

"It's okay, take your time. I know you can do it." I petted her mane.

Biscuit turned around and took a few steps back. My first instinct was to hold on to her reins, but I knew better than that. Biscuit wasn't flighty. I trusted her and that she wouldn't run away. I held my breath as she darted straight for the red rock. Her horn met the stone with a loud clank. I winced, expecting blood to explode from her horn. However, to my surprise, I discovered that she was not only fine, but that the blue light had intensified. The red rock behind it vanished, leaving a blue archway in its place.

"Quick, before it closes." I mounted Biscuit's saddle while Philip swung himself onto Ace's saddle, sliding in front of Julian.

We galloped through the archway. A stinging sensation went through my head, pressure compressed my skull, and wind blasted me from all sides. Like the previous time, the unpleasantness stopped abruptly, and we found ourselves back in the forest.

"What should we do with him?" I pointed at Julian.

Philip heaved Julian off the horse and lay him on the grass. "If you don't mind, I'm going to leave him here. I'm sure he'll be fine. He managed to follow us. He'll find a way back home."

A proper princess would never allow that to happen. She would insist on bringing a foreign prince, even one as rude as Julian, to safety. But I was running out of time, and after the way Julian had talked to Philip and me and mistreated Biscuit, I didn't feel obligated to do anything for him.

"Agreed. We'll leave him here." I threw the yarn ball in front of me and followed down the path it took us.

The sun rose slowly, turning the sky a soft shade of blush

and illuminating Philip's bronze skin and verdant eyes. I smiled at him. To everyone else I was either a pitiful cursed princess or a reckless young girl, but Philip didn't judge me. I didn't have to explain myself to him. He knew me. With him I was happy, weightless, and blessed.

🎕 15 🎕

GRISELDA

As it turned out, the first river ship wasn't going all the way to Vienna, a blessing in disguise since it allowed me to switch in Belgrade to a vacationer boat, which didn't stink like fish and had much better food. I hid amongst the rich travelers, stealing rich cheeses, cakes, dried fruits, and chocolate pralines, not minding in the least gaining a dress size. Discovering that dress-cleaning services were provided on the ship, I snuck into the washing room and stole a few garments. I discarded my ugly, scratchy prison clothes and covered my skin in fancy velvets, silks, and brocades.

See, Mother, in less than a week, I transformed from a prisoner to a noblewoman. Not long now and I'll be empress just as you had always wanted for me.

My new living conditions made time pass faster, and soon we reached Budapest. I was so close to the Inverse Kingdom, to meeting with the seven-headed Mouse King, I practically tasted sweet victory and was certain nothing could go wrong.

As it turned out, I was mistaken. Perhaps my happiness had jinxed my luck. After all, Mother had always told me that one should never get too comfortable in a joyful state.

I didn't know immediately that something was off as we left Budapest. It was only about half an hour into the journey that I heard a squeaking noise that sounded like unoiled hinges. What had we picked up in Hungary? My stupidity and curiosity led me to shift into a mouse and investigate.

When I lay eyes on the monsters in the metal cages, my hind legs trembled, my ears went down, and my breathing turned quick and shallow. A dozen cats were released. Judging by the slow and groggy way they moved, they had been sedated with calming herbs before being transported. Aware that the effects of medicine would wear off soon, I rushed up the stairs and out onto the deck, away from the felines to consider my options. One look at the fast-moving, wide river confirmed my fears. I wouldn't survive a swim. I was trapped on a ship with cats, my next stop being days away.

Whether my stealing of food had been noticed, or whether cats were brought onto ships routinely, I didn't know. Either way, my days of carelessness were over. From now on, I would have to time each shift carefully, ensuring the humans didn't see my girl form while the cats didn't catch me in my mouse form.

Not bothering to shift back into a human, I hurried to the kitchen to stock up on food.

I was too late. Through the hole underneath the door, I saw the new guards. Two fat, gray cats with yellow eyes and creepy slit pupils lay on either end of the room. Worse, both were next to my hiding places, as if they could sniff the residual mouse smell and hoped to smoke me out.

I pivoted around, planning to get my food from the cafeteria when footsteps neared me, and a female maid exclaimed, "A mouse! A mouse! Taz, get her!"

Taz didn't turn out to be a waiter, a cook, or a sailor. Taz was a cat twice the size of the felines inside the storage room and fast as a whip. He darted down the corridor and pounced at me while the maid stomped her feet, bringing one of her heavy wooden shoes down on my tail.

I screeched in pain but didn't allow myself to examine my poor tail. Instead, I dashed away as fast as I could, the cat gaining on me. He leaped in the air, and then he was in front of me, blocking my way. His eyes flashed with bloodlust. His claw shot out and swiped my side, and the smell of copper filled the air as hot liquid trickled down my body. He swiped again at me, but this time, I was quicker to avoid him. I danced away from him until my body was pressed against the wall. Just when I thought this was it, that I would have to shift into a human and reveal what I was, I spotted a tiny hole in the door a foot away from me. With everything I had, I sprinted for it and jostled my body into the opening. The cat's sharp claw whizzed past my head, scratching my ear. Bleeding, I pressed myself inside the hole.

The cat pushed his paw into the small space, less than half an inch away from my body. My heart hammered so fast, I was surprised it was still inside my chest.

After a few minutes, the cat removed his claws, but his yellow eyes continued to stare at me. Knowing I couldn't stay like this forever, I searched for a way out of my dilemma. Really, I had only one choice, destroy the wood between me and the other room. How I wished I could access my dark power. Alas, I had spent it all to create the nutcracker curse and widen the portal from Snake Island to Schönbrunn, leaving my magic reserves depleted for the next few months.

The only tools at my disposal were my teeth, which had been softened by the fresh cheese and sweets of the last week. My incisors protested as I bit into the hard wood, and my gums bled, but I pressed on, reminding myself that breaking or ripping out my teeth would be much less painful than death by hunger and thirst, or ending up as a cat's toy.

You could've avoided all of this, if you had only been more careful.

Mother's voice taunted me. I messed up. Like I always did. Annoyed with myself, I bit down harder on the wood. A snapping sound came from my mouth, and then an overwhelming ache shot up into my gum, mouth, and head, making me want to drop to the floor and cry. Instead, I pushed on, chomping through the wood, even as a bloody tooth fell out of my mouth. When my whole face was on fire, I paused for a few breaths before resuming my work. Finally, my efforts paid off, and I was able to see into the room on the other side. A simple cabin with two bunk beds. Spurred on by my success, I continued to destroy the wood, widening the hole until I fit through.

The delicious smell of cheese entered my nostrils, and every part of my body screamed to go for it. It was only my human brain that allowed me to withstand the temptation and avoid getting caught in the mousetrap. However, not being able to eat the only food I saw in the cabin was pure torture and made me certain I would go insane if I had to smell it for longer than a few minutes.

When a maid ambled into the room, wearing an apron with big pockets, I knew this was my chance to be transported away from the mousetrap.

I took a deep breath and darted across the floor, realizing my mistake too late. A silver metal cylinder flashed in front of my vision and then came down hard, trapping me with a deafening, tinkling sound. My surroundings turned pitch black as I was captured in the metal bowl. I closed my eyes and stopped moving, trying to conserve what little energy I had to figure out how to survive. There had to be a way out of this. I hadn't come this far to die. The maid would slip up, and I would run for my life. If luck was on my side, I might even regain enough energy to shift back into a human.

"I captured a mouse. I captured a mouse. What do I do now?" the pathetic maid mumbled to herself, as if she was solving a complicated problem no one had ever encountered before her.

"I should get one of the men to take care of it. Yes, that's a good idea," she said to herself, opening and closing the door with two clicks.

Despite my exhausted state, I forced myself to calculate how much time I had. I judged that while a mouse wouldn't be classified as an emergency, the combination of the hysterical maid and a sailor wanting to play a hero meant somebody would come in the next five minutes to dispose of me. Once they did, there would be no hope for me. I would either be thrown overboard to drown or fed to the cats.

Thus, even though pain radiated down every inch of my body, and my skull was about to split, I focused my mind, willing myself to shift back into a human. A groan came out of my maw, and my muscles trembled. I pushed through the ache, reminding myself that there was no way I would survive unless I shifted into my human form.

No other shift had ever felt as impossible as this one. I was completely drained, and wet tears streamed down my snout while my teeth ground against each other. Finally, my mind won out over my body. The metal bowl on top of me trembled and then flew off me just as the door handle was pushed down.

The maid had returned, and with her was a bulky sailor, who carried a cat. The sailor threw down the cat and cursed at the sight of me while the maid screamed, "What sorcery is this!"

My body went on autopilot, and I hurled the bowl at the maid, eliciting a scream, kicked the cat as hard as I could, and chopped my hand into the sailor's throat. He stumbled backward, gasping for air while the maid darted away from me.

I hurried out of the cabin, darted down the corridor, and reached the cleaning supply room undetected. Inside, I crawled into a large empty storage box, which would have to serve as my bed while I recovered from the events of tonight and figured out how to stay undetected as a human. If Delilah could see me in my sorry state, my body bruised, my mouth bleeding, she would laugh. If she were here, she wouldn't hide in the filthy supply room, but seduce a passenger into sharing his cabin with her. Alas, I wasn't Delilah. And since it was no longer safe for me to shift into my mouse form, I would have to spend the rest of my trip in this tiny space that smelt of vinegar.

As I lay in the wooden box, marinating in the tart scent, my gums bleeding, my teeth aching, and my body trembling with hunger and exhaustion, I swore to myself that I would take everything from Clara and the emperor just as they had from me and Mother. I would torture them just as they had tortured Mother and me. They had put me into this forsaken situation and were responsible for every miserable moment in my life and for Mother's death, and I would punish them tenfold for everything I and Mother had suffered.

❧ 16 ❧

CLARA

My adventures in the desert and the exhausting horseback ride left my clothing dusty, causing it to cling to my sweat-covered body. Thus, when a beautiful lake opened in front of me to my left, I couldn't resist its call. Hastily, I dismounted Biscuit, scooped up the golden ball of yarn, and proclaimed, "I need a bath."

I hurried to the lake without glancing back at Philip, not wanting to hear that a bath was a bad idea. Also, I didn't want him to see my inflamed cheeks, a byproduct of me imagining him diving into the lake, then coming back up with pearls of water glistening on his skin and hair. I wanted to shake myself. What was happening to me? Was that what the girls at court meant when they said there comes a time when you do want to get married and be with a man? No, that couldn't be it, because while I had strange thoughts about Philip, I was more certain than ever that I did not want to get married.

Leaving the palace had showed me how much there was outside of Schönbrunn's walls. I might not be able to explore all the world in my lifetime, but I needed to explore at least some before I was ready to bind myself to someone and be stuck in a castle, produce heirs, and throw balls for the court and foreign kingdoms. Just thinking about these responsibilities made my stomach roil. Perhaps that was how every young woman felt about marriage. If so, why didn't anyone talk about it? Why were those feelings ignored and subdued? I wanted to shout them out into the world—loud and clear, for everyone to hear.

"Are you all right?"

I pivoted and squinted at Philip, the sun behind him blinding me.

"You've been standing in front of the lake for a few minutes. Did you change your mind about bathing?"

"No, that's not it. I was just thinking." I studied him, considering how much to reveal. It would have been easy to keep my sentiments to myself, but then hadn't I just thought how freeing it would be to speak them out loud? Didn't I owe it to myself and my best friend to be honest?

"I don't want to marry any of the princes, and I'm not interested in giving them heirs or entertaining foreign delegations."

Philip cracked a smile. "I wouldn't want to produce heirs with Julian, Simon, Leon, or Felix either."

I grinned. "Is that so? You don't consider them excellent choices?"

Philip snorted. "Simon would eat and drink himself to death in a few short years, and he has no idea about strategy or foreign affairs. Julian is too concerned with strategy. Felix would squeeze the kingdom dry, doubling the tax in his first year. And Leon, well, I guess I wouldn't want my spouse to flirt with the whole court."

The last sentence elicited a gasp from me. I agreed with Philip's assessment of Simon, Julian, and Felix. But his evaluation of Leon... "You're being harsh. Just because Leon is good-looking and charming—"

"So, you don't mind the idea of giving him heirs?" Philip's voice lost all playfulness and turned as hard as gravel.

"I don't know how I feel about him. I would need more time to get to know him. But from those four, he seems like the lesser evil," I answered cautiously.

Philip grimaced. "Is that what you want in a husband? One that isn't too bad? Don't you have higher—"

"Standards?" I interrupted, inhaling deeply and puffing out my chest. "Yes, I have standards. But I'm also a princess. I have pressures you won't ever understand."

"I'm sorry. I didn't mean—"

"It's not about what I want but about what the kingdom needs. Father won't allow me to remain unmarried and bring shame on him, on us. What I just said makes me a bad princess and a bad daughter. A useless daughter." I wriggled my hands in the water, watching it ripple, unable to keep looking at Philip.

"No, it doesn't. It makes you, you. And for what it's worth, I like you just the way you are." Philip must have sensed that even though his words were sweet, he couldn't lift the heaviness that rested on my shoulders, so he changed his tactic. "Why don't we focus on what you want to do, instead of what you don't want to do? Is there anything you want to do?"

I undid my braid and pulled my hair into a messy bun unbecoming a princess. "Yes, I want to see the world. I want to travel. Go on adventures. Explore." I turned to him, adrenaline pumping through me. "And right now, I want to race you into the water."

Before I could second-guess myself, I unbuttoned my cloak and threw it onto the ground. Then I shucked off my riding dress and boots, trying to tell myself there was nothing wrong with doing so. After all, if I went swimming in all my clothes, they would get wet and give me a cold. Much better to flash a bit of skin than to die from pneumonia. Wearing only my white undershirt and underpants that scandalously reached to the middle of my thigh, I dashed toward the lake. I didn't know whether I was trying to impress Philip or myself, but I was determined not to go into the lake slowly, cringing at every cold inch that covered my body. So instead, I pulled my arms high in front of me and, when I was in waist-deep, I dived, submerging myself fully and allowing the water to wash away the dust from my skin and cleanse my hair.

When I got back up, Philip was next to me, a big smile on his face. "I needed this. So refreshing."

"Me too. I'm full of great ideas, aren't I?"

He splashed me with water. "Don't get too full of yourself, Princess."

I splashed him back. "Never!"

"Do you promise?" He splashed me harder, and I returned the gesture, squealing, "yes."

Soon, he had captured my hands, preventing me from splashing him further. Only a few inches separated our faces. My breath became heavier and slower. Despite the cool lake, I was burning up. And it didn't get better when Philip pushed back my wet hair to reveal my flaming cheeks or leaned closer. "Tell me, if you want me to stop," he breathed.

"I don't want you to stop." I closed the distance between us and pressed my lips against his. His mouth opened tentatively, and my tongue met his. Dove wings fluttered in my stomach, and a pleasant tingle spread from my core into every inch of my body. The sensations were odd and took getting used to but were delightful in their strangeness. If anyone saw us like this, they would decide that what we were doing was wrong. Yet, I wasn't worried about others' opinions or bothered by my critical voice warning me this wouldn't end well, because kissing Philip felt so utterly right. Unfortunately, we couldn't press stop on time, and when the moment was over, we both pulled back. I stared at Philip, silently willing him to tell me what this meant, how much this would change everything. As my excitement vanished, I wondered if I had made a horrible mistake, destroying the only true friendship I had.

I opened my mouth several times to speak, but no words came out. Philip continued to look at me, his face going from happy, to concerned, to worried, to deep in thought.

A loud popping sound tore my attention away from Philip and toward Biscuit and Ace. Our horses were no longer alone. One of the princes stood in between them. I dashed out of the water, my embarrassment at being clothed in nothing besides wet undergarments pushed aside by my need to check out what I thought was a mirage. But as I got closer, the prince who had arrived out of nowhere remained. He looked as surprised as I felt, even though it was him who had suddenly appeared out of thin air.

"What are you doing here, Simon?" I asked.

❦ 17 ❦

CLARA

"I ... I...," Simon stammered and wrung his hands. "I bought a tracking spell, which promised to find you and bring me to you." He looked from me to Biscuit, Ace, and Philip. "And I guess it worked." Simon smiled nervously. For somebody who had achieved something he had wanted, he didn't look happy. He took in the birch trees, the meadow, and the lake. "Where are we? Where's the next town?"

"I don't know," I answered truthfully while wondering how to get rid of him.

Simon scratched his head. "I was worried about you. Felix and Julian went after you immediately when it was discovered that you were missing. Leon too." He twisted a thick ring on his chubby finger. "I stayed at the castle. I thought it was better for me to wait for you to return to the castle, but then you didn't. Everyone got more and more worried as time passed. The emperor said the guards who had been charged with the night shift when you slipped out would be executed."

I inhaled sharply. "He can't do that."

Philip grimaced. "Yes, he can. He's the king. And you're his only child."

Simon shrugged apologetically. "Anyway, I couldn't just sit around. And my mother sent me a letter owl, telling me to stop being useless and follow you," he admitted sheepishly.

As bad as I felt for Simon and the pressure he seemed to be under to pursue me, I knew immediately this journey wasn't right for him. With Julian, I had feared he might betray us, but with Simon I worried he would slow us down. Already, he was tugging on his clothes and glancing nervously around. He would be much more comfortable at the closest pub, filling his stomach, rather than going on a strenuous journey.

"You have to return to Schönbrunn or your own kingdom, Simon," I said as gently as I could. "I need to find the Crackatook. It won't be an easy task, and I don't think you're up for that."

He raised his hands halfway up, then dropped them. "Perhaps I could help."

"The last being we met was a magical scorpion who gave us a riddle to solve. If we failed, he would have paralyzed us with his poison and allowed his scorpion friends to feast on us."

My words had their intended effect, and Simon's ruddy cheeks drained of color.

"Right. I guess I should return to my kingdom." Simon motioned to Philip, Ace, and Biscuit. "It seems like you have everything under control without me."

Guilt built inside of me at the dejected expression on Simon's face. I felt even worse when I realized he had no idea how to get out of the forest, his head swiveling left and right, his eyes getting bigger and bigger by the second and filling with tears.

"We'll help you find the next village," I said just as there was a chime and the nutcracker in my bag opened his mouth and said, "Only eight more days remain. If you don't solve the curse, you'll turn into a wooden doll and your soul will be locked for all eternity inside of me."

My gut clenched. I had lost another day.

Simon glanced between the nutcracker and me, his jaw going slack. "That's why you went to search for the Crackatook yourself." The shock on his face told me he still didn't understand my decision completely but no longer thought me certifiable. I didn't really care what his opinion of me was, but I didn't want him to blab. Simon didn't exactly seem like someone who could keep a secret, and I had the bad suspicion that a few glasses of wine would make him spill his guts.

"You must promise not to tell anyone about what is on the line if I don't break the curse, or we won't take you to a village," I said, hating that I had to exploit his fears.

"Of course." He bobbed his head quickly, and I relaxed a fraction.

With my undergarments half dried, I put my riding dress over them, not caring about my display of unladylike behavior in front of Simon. He had already seen too much. It was too late to try and uphold the charade of the well-behaved, prudent, and obedient princess I wasn't.

"Do you know where a village is?" Philip asked quietly so that only I could hear.

"No, but we'll find one. We can't just leave him here."

Philip pinched the space between his brows. "He should have never come."

"No, but that's not reason enough to let him die out here."

"All right. But we better hurry before time runs out."

I took out the nutcracker and stared at his impassive face. If I didn't get the Crackatook in time, this would become me. A shiver rushed through me, making goose bumps explode on my skin. I wished Philip would hold me, tell me everything would be all right, but neither was a good idea with Simon around, so I simply petted Biscuit before swinging myself into the saddle.

"I don't have a horse," Simon said.

I gave Philip a questioning look, and he muttered, "Just so that you know, Ace is expecting a big reward for when all of this is over."

I petted Ace's head. "Good boy."

Despite his evident displeasure, Philip helped Simon to get into the saddle, then mounted Ace himself, sliding to the front. Simon hugged Philip's torso, and I put Biscuit into a canter, hoping the wind would hide my rumbling laugh at the sight of Simon clutching Philip tightly.

I petted Biscuit's white-gold mane. "Take us to the nearest village." I wasn't sure whether she could do that, but I had to put my hope in her since the golden ball of yarn would only take me to the next magical kingdom and not the next village.

We rode for only an hour when a small town came into view, its evening street lamps and outdoor pub lights greeting us. Somehow, Simon had managed to fall asleep on the horse and was snoring loudly. Philip poked him in the ribs, and Simon startled. "What? What's going on?"

"We're here." Philip dismounted Ace and helped Simon out of the saddle. "Don't come after us again," he said sternly.

"Oh, don't worry, he won't," a silky voice said.

I whirled around to find Felix approaching with guards, who wore a uniform with the Serbian crest—two white eagles on a red background.

"Lock away the abductor," Felix commanded his guards, pointing at Philip. "I'll take care of the princess."

Philip didn't have time to resist the arrest. Within seconds, he was handcuffed and dragged away. When his eyes met mine, I mouthed, "I'll get you out." Then I jabbed my finger into Simon's chest. "Did you plan this? Were you working with Felix?"

Felix snorted. "Him? This nitwit can barely put two and two together."

I narrowed my eyes at Felix. "What did you do?"

He gave a self-indulgent smile. "It was easy. After I lost you at the magic village, I was planning to return to Vienna and report to your father that you ran off with a guard. But then Simon appeared, telling the griffins he was there to buy a tracking spell. I waited until he was done and approached the griffins a second time, showing them a bag of coins, and saying that I too would like a tracking spell. After bartering with the vendor, I ended up paying only half price since I argued that it was easier to produce a spell to track a person the sorcerer had just met. I returned to Vienna, gathered my guards, and used the spell, making the correct assumption that it didn't matter if I followed Simon immediately. As you can see, I was right."

I screamed on the inside, wanting to hit Felix's smug face, but knowing I had to control myself if I wanted a chance to free Philip.

Simon's lower lip trembled, and he looked close to tears.

Felix puffed his chest out. "What are you looking at? Go! Unless you want to be locked up too." Simon scurried away while Felix grabbed my arm roughly. "We'll need to get you into an inn, Your Highness, until your carriage is ready to bring you back to Schönbrunn." He pulled out a torn envelope and shoved it into my hand. "From your Father."

I gasped at the owl post. "How did you get it?" Owls only delivered letters to the intended person, and if they couldn't find the recipient, they returned to the castle.

Felix gave me a crooked smile. "The stupid owl kept

circling outside Gumpoldskirchen. It was easy to put an arrow into it."

My hands trembled with rage. "You killed an innocent animal?"

Felix shrugged. "I got you the letter. That's what matters."

I was too furious to ask why he had bothered giving it to me after reading it himself. As Felix dragged me behind himself, I stomped loudly, wanting him to think me a spoiled princess and underestimate me, so that my future escape would be easier, all the while keeping an eye out for guards who wore the Austrian crest—two black eagles on a white background. Unfortunately, I didn't see any. The village was too small to warrant stationed guards.

Felix took me into a two-story inn with flowered wallpaper and demanded the most secure room. He led me upstairs and practically shoved me into the tiny chamber equipped with nothing more than a small bed and a bathing basin.

"Give me your weapons."

When I didn't follow his command, he clicked his tongue.

"Do you want me to search you for weapons?"

With a heavy sigh, I discarded my coat slowly, grateful the scorpion's paralyzation venom and the nutcracker were hidden inside the invisible bag. Then I handed Felix my dagger and took off my boots to show I wasn't hiding any weapons there.

"Good. I'll be back for you soon." Felix left before I could reply.

I wanted to throw myself into the pillow and weep. Since that wouldn't help my situation, I stepped to the sink and splashed my face with icy water. "You can do this, Clara," I reassured myself as I concocted a plan.

❧ 18 ❧

CLARA

Even though I knew I wouldn't find anything reassuring, I couldn't resist reading Father's letter.

Dear Clara,

I hope this letter reaches you before it is too late. I don't know what you were thinking, going after the Crackatook by yourself, but I beg you to return. There's nothing you can do, and the palace is the only safe place for you.

I can't bear the idea of losing you. Whatever your plans are please reconsider.

Your Father

Hot tears streamed down my face. Once again, I was disappointing Father. Why couldn't I be the princess and daughter he wanted me to be? I had kept telling myself that the distress my disappearance had caused would be worth it in the end once I broke the curse. But what if failed? What if I had forgone the last twelve days I could've spent with my only family to chase an impossible goal?

The housekeeper, who brought me a meal of chicken and potatoes, didn't comment on my tears. Once she picked up my empty food tray, I lay in bed, waiting for the inn to grow quiet. Despite the letter, despite my doubts, I wasn't willing to give up. I would see this through. And if I chose to return to the palace before the twelve days were up, I would do it of my own accord, and not because Felix dragged me back.

Even though he had transformed into a crazy person, I didn't believe he would tear me out of bed in the middle of the night and shove me into a carriage. That type of action might not go over too well with the future father-in-law he was trying to impress. Because of this, I decided I was safe for the night, but Philip wasn't. I needed to figure out where Felix's men had put Philip.

I wasn't foolish enough to think I could escape through the door. If guards hadn't been posted right outside of my room, I was certain they were on the staircase, prepared to stop me if I made a run for it.

The window, however, was a different story. I had cracked it open earlier, ensuring I wouldn't have to do so later and make unnecessary noise. I stared at my path to freedom. Jumping would result, in a best-case scenario, in a twisted ankle, in a worst-case scenario, a broken leg, rendering me helpless and useless to Philip.

What I needed was a rope. I stripped the bed of its sheets and tied them together, praying the knots would hold my weight and not come apart. Then I tied one end to the bedpost and threw the other out of the window. I waited a few seconds for someone to raise the alarm. When no one did, I checked one last time that I had all my belongings and took a deep breath, swung my legs out of the window, and hung on to the makeshift rope as I maneuvered my way down the stone wall. When my feet hit the ground, I glanced furtively around me, expecting lamps to illuminate my face and guards to cuff me. But nothing of that sort happened. I allowed myself a big smile and a moment of happiness until I realized the hard part was still ahead of me. Not only did I need to free Philip, Biscuit, and Ace, I needed to locate them first.

Since it would be hard to control both horses and they would likely attract attention, I decided to start with Philip. Given the town's small size, it wasn't hard to find the building where Philip was held, especially because it was the only one with a Serbian guard positioned outside it.

Since walking in through the front door was out of the question, I gave the building a wide berth and approached it from the back.

My heart picked up a notch as I spotted the top of a barred window, most of it hidden by the street. I kneeled in front of it and whispered, "Philip. Are you in there?"

There was a pause and then a creaking sound. Familiar green eyes met mine, and my heart clenched as I took in Philip's face. It was black and blue and swollen on one side, while his other cheek sported a long diagonal cut and dried blood.

"What have they done to you?" I choked out as he said, "Clara, what are you doing here?"

I pulled myself together, knowing it was my time to be the strong one. "Getting you out of here, obviously." I wrapped my hands around the bars and pulled.

"That's futile. You won't be able to rip them out."

"I won't. But Biscuit and Ace might. Do you know where they are?"

He shook his head. "My guess is they were taken to some stables."

"All right." I stood up from my crouch. "I'll be right back."

"What? No. Clara, you can't do that."

I gave him the most reassuring smile I could muster. "I

can, and I will. You would do the same for me if the roles were reversed."

Once again, the small size of the town proved to be advantageous, and I soon discovered the stable. With no one posted outside, I was able to slip inside and made my way down the stalls, but a familiar voice soon brought me to a standstill.

"That's not enough," Felix said. "She's a unicorn. She's worth much more."

I clenched my hands into fists and my neck tensed. Was he seriously trying to sell my beloved unicorn, which had been given to me by my dead mother? How was he planning to explain this to my father? Would he lie about Biscuit going missing, maybe even blame Philip for her disappearance?

"Fine. Fine. I'll add something. I'll get you an emerald on top of the ruby," the other man said.

"Good. But I need to see it first before agreeing. Get it now and hurry. I don't have all night."

I had just enough time to press myself against another stable, hiding my face as the buyer hurried past me.

Since Felix wasn't leaving, and my chances were better to fight one man rather than two, I picked up a hoof knife and tiptoed toward Biscuit's stable. My stomach cramped as I took in Felix leaning casually against the wall while Biscuit puffed her nostrils and stamped her front hoof.

"I can't wait to get rid of you, you stupid beast," he said, making me certain he would have hit her if she had been a smaller animal. My disgust for Felix tripled, but even so, I couldn't bring myself to aim the knife for his neck, so instead, I went for a nonlethal spot, his shoulder. Just before I could bring the weapon down on him, Felix pivoted around, and our eyes met, his widening in shock. He jumped aside, and the knife hit his jacket, slicing through it and the top layer of his skin, barely enough to elicit a few blood drops.

"How the hell did you get out?"

I didn't reply. Instead, I charged him again, this time, aiming for his chest. Unfortunately, I had lost my surprise factor, and Felix turned out to be better at this than me. He stopped my arm midair with ease and twisted my wrist hard, forcing me to release the knife. The blade clattered to the ground, and I shoved my knee full-force into his groin. His face contorted in pain, and he let out a yowl. I had to make a split decision—injure him further or free Biscuit. Even though the second scenario was riskier, I didn't want to hurt a man already down on the ground, so I flung open the stall and jumped on Biscuit, glad she was still saddled and bridled. As we were leaving, Felix got up, clutching the knife he had twisted out of my hand earlier. I panicked, terrified that he would hurt Biscuit, but she remained calm and pulled down her head so that her horn was pointing at him. A light came out of it, and Felix was blasted against the wall behind him. His body made a sickening crunch as he collapsed.

"Good girl," I said to Biscuit, mesmerized by her new trick. "Where's Ace?"

She neighed and charged forward, making me fear she hadn't heard me in her state of adrenaline high, but then she paused in front of the last stall by the door, and Ace's dark, silky mane came into view. My hands reached to open his stall as a voice shouted, "What are you doing? Thief, thief!"

The buyer had returned.

"Can you repeat your horn trick?" I asked Biscuit as Ace joined us. She lowered her head and white light came out of her horn and blasted the man backward, making him land hard on his behind.

We galloped past him, and I prayed we would be long gone by the time Felix's guards arrived.

I took a back alley toward Philip, who was waiting at the window for me.

"You did it." He glanced with awe between me, Biscuit, and Ace.

"I told you I would." I pulled out a rope Philip had smartly brought along and that was still in Ace's saddle bag. Once the rope was wound around Philip's prison bar and Biscuit's and Ace's saddles, I yelled, "Pull!"

The horses darted forward, and the bars groaned and shifted.

"Again!"

The horses had to repeat the procedure three more times until the bars were flung out of the window. I took a stone. "Step back." Philip pushed as far away from the window as possible, and I flung the stone. The window exploded into shards, and Philip climbed out.

"Are you all right?" I searched his body for cuts.

He grinned up at me. "You might have saved me, but I'm not that helpless, Princess." He swung into Ace's saddle as Felix's men hurried toward us.

Philip and I pushed Ace and Biscuit into a gallop. Luckily for us, the Serbian guards had come sans horses, and the Vienna Forest was next to the village, allowing us to disappear into its thick darkness.

I relaxed into the ride, a smile curling my lips. The relief at our successful escape, however, didn't last long. The nutcracker chimed against my cloak and spoke in his eerie voice, "Only seven more days remain. If you don't solve the curse, you'll turn into a wooden doll and your soul will be locked for all eternity inside of me."

"How is this possible? Another day couldn't have passed that quickly. We weren't even in a magical realm." Desperation rose within me, threatening to drag me into its depth.

Philip took my hand and gave me a reassuring look that I could tell was for my benefit. "We'll be fine. We still have seven days."

"You're right," I said, trying not to think too much about how awful my life would be if I ended up trapped in a wooden shell and the guilt I would feel for not saying goodbye to Father.

❦ 19 ❦

GRISELDA

The ship slowed as it approached Vienna, signaling the end of my journey. Rising above the other buildings, the cream-colored St. Charles Church came into view in all its baroque glory. A dome the shade of teal was centered between two columns that were each surrounded by tower pavilions.

While I had managed to hide in my human form on the ship, there was no way I could get off the ship as a girl. I had to transform into a mouse and pray I would be faster than the cats.

Not knowing whether the felines would be allowed to roam freely on the ship or would be locked away while the passengers debarked, I grew more and more restless as the ship crawled to a standstill. I didn't want to be one of the first ones to debark, but neither did I want to be one of the last ones. My gut told me the cats would either get off at the beginning or the end.

I clasped my hands together in a prayer, asking whoever was listening to not let me die after I had come so far, and then I transformed. My body became tiny, my claws and ears grew, and whiskers and a tail sprouted from my body. After not shifting for a several days, it took me a few minutes to adjust to my transformation and remember where I was and what I needed to do. Once I did, I raced through the wooden hole in the door and into the corridor.

The corridor appeared to be empty. All I needed to do was get to the end of it, up the stairs, across the deck, and over the bridge, which would deliver me onto the land. *It's going to be easy,* I told myself, running as fast as I could down the corridor. Sharp claws whizzed an inch past my eye, almost ripping it out. Instead of panicking at the cat's claw, I pushed myself, dashing up the stairs. The cat was behind me, gaining on me. I reached the deck and weaved in between the passengers, who hadn't noticed me yet but yelled at the cat darting underneath their feet.

Mercifully, the humans acted as a shield, slowing the feline. I remained undiscovered until I crossed the bridge connecting the ship to the port.

"A mouse!" a servant shouted, and three men chased after me, almost pushing me off the bridge and into the water. I ducked this and that way, pressing on, and luckily, the sailors lost interest in me when it became clear I was leaving their ship.

I didn't take a break when I reached the port, afraid the cat might still be coming after me. It was only once I was far away from the port and deep into the city that I allowed myself to stop and take deep breaths as I mulled over my next problem. How was I going to find the Inverse Kingdom? I had been certain my mouse senses would get me to the seven-headed Mouse King, but I could hardly travel on foot or in mouse form if I wanted to arrive before Clara.

What I needed was a horse. The problem was that, in

addition to stealing one, I would have to remember how to ride one, something I hadn't done in the last ten years I had been locked up.

Since I had no other choice, I transformed into my human form and marched down Operngasse, a busy street lined with restaurants and bars reeking of sausage and beer. If I were Delilah or my mother, I would use my charm to get help from the passersby. Since I didn't have any charm, I tried to stay away from people and not attract any attention. After walking for five minutes, I came across a pub that had an unattended horse outside of it. The horse was saddled, bridled, and was on the smaller side, which I preferred since it would be easier for me to mount.

Glancing both ways, I made sure no one was watching me. Then I untied the horse and pushed one foot into the stirrup and swung my other leg across its torso, delighted when I managed to rise onto it on my first try.

"What are you doing?" A man with a ruddy face stormed out of the pub.

I hit the horse in the flanks hard, forcing it into a gallop. Panic gripped me as the mare ran faster and faster. I gripped the bridle, knowing my life depended on it. If caught, I would go back to jail, and if I fell off the horse, I would break my spine and then go to jail. My heart hammered, and my legs and hands locked in a death grip. Adrenaline pumped through me, obliterating everything besides my need to leave the city. It was only when we hit the paved roads, which gave way to the forest that I exhaled, my back slumping with relief.

I galloped for what felt like an eternity until finally there was a shift in my surroundings. To my human eye everything looked the same, but the mouse shifter in me sensed the nearness of a portal to the Inverse Kingdom.

I dismounted the horse and stepped toward two big trees,

whose branches leaned toward each other, as if forming an archway. Once the portal sensed my energy and that I belonged, it glowed a blue light and permitted me entry. I stepped through and gasped as a transformation overtook my body. My weight shifted to my hind legs, which bent at a strange angle, and claws grew from my hands. I touched my behind and found a long, skinny tail. My ears were rounded, and whiskers were sprouting from the tip of my nose. The Inverse Kingdom had turned me into a strange combination between a mouse and a human.

In front of me was a bubbling azure lake, a simple wooden boat perched on the shore. In the middle of the lake stood a hill, a gray castle with tall spires and towers built atop of it. Stepping toward the lake, I wanted to take in my new reflection, but couldn't since steam rose from the burbling water. I wasn't particularly keen to travel over a boiling lake, but I had no other choice. I needed the Mouse King's help.

Careful, I climbed into the boat and rowed, straining my arms and shoulders. Only a few minutes in, I was covered in sweat and blisters, courtesy of the scalding, spewing lake.

I got as close to the boulder as I could, which wasn't close enough to completely avoid the lake. I jumped out of the boat and winced as my feet and ankles were scalded through my shoes and clothes. Although I shoved the boat up the boulder so it wouldn't float away, it glided back to the other shore. Stupid magic. I hobbled around the boulder, waiting for my skin to stop feeling like it was melting so I could focus fully on the next task.

Don't be such a baby. A few blisters won't kill you, Mother's voice played in my head.

Spurred on by it, I hobbled halfway around the boulder, and a fiery entrance came into view. The eight-foot-tall, flaming archway made my hands shake and my throat constrict, but I saw no other entry. Taking a deep breath, I went on my hands and knees, deciding that crawling was the safest way to make it through the passageway unharmed. However, as soon as the flames surrounded me, a soothing mist engulfed me, alleviating my earlier burns. I bathed in it for a minute, mesmerized by how flames in this kingdom were cool water, while water was singeing lava. When I exited the flaming archway, I found myself inside the courtyard, a tall maze separating me from the castle. I wasn't too concerned about figuring my way out of the labyrinth, certain my shifter senses would guide me. However, I did worry what awaited me between the hedges.

I entered the maze and had to choose between going to the left or the right. On a whim, I chose left, reassuring myself it didn't matter where I went in the beginning, it was what I did once I was inside the maze. After seven steps, I was given the choice to either continue straight or turn to the left. I turned, and a whooshing sounded behind me. When I pivoted around, I discovered a tall metal wall had fallen behind me, blocking off the path I had come from. In front of me, a maze of red lights crisscrossed from one hedge to the other. I swallowed hard, having the bad feeling that touching one of the lights would mean excruciating pain, if not worse. Taking a deep breath, I stepped over the first light line and ducked under the next. That wasn't too hard. Something sprayed from above, covering me in a sweet mist. I swayed, and my shoulder touched a light. A lightning shock went through my body.

"Aargh!" The pain jolted my mind awake, making me realize that whatever was in the mist that came from above was addling my reflexes. I needed to hurry and inhale as little as possible of the tainted air unless I wanted to die by lightening. Pointing my toes, stretching my legs, and extending my arms, I maneuvered my way down the maze, crawling, jumping, and back bending my way from one light line to the next. And yet, I received shock after shock against my legs, arms, torso, whiskers, and long tail. My nerve endings screamed in agony, and my heart was leaping in my chest.

The sweet mist kept sprinkling from above. It was every-where. *Sit down. Lie down. Relax,* it whispered, and my aching, heavy limbs wanted to obey.

I pinched my arm hard and slapped my cheek. "Focus, you have to focus." I tore my eyes wide open and crawled below the line in front of me, then jumped across the next. My tail hit the line, and a jolt snapped through me. I ignored the tears and sweat running down my face and pressed on, trying my very best to not hit any more lines. And yet one jolt after another went through my body, raining down on me, punishing me hard. Pain was part of me, and I was part of the pain. My chest burned, my limbs were a trembling mess, and my eyes ticked nervously.

I couldn't think. I couldn't see. What was I trying to do again? Who cared? I would never make it out alive. Ready to sink into the soft grass underneath my feet, I lifted my head, which felt like an iron ball ready to split in half, for a final time and found the exit in front of me. Only three light lines. I could do this.

The first light line was so low to the ground, I had to press myself flat against the grass and barely move as I crawled. The second line split into two—one high, the other low. I had to jump in between them, which I managed, but my back hit the upper line, and pain exploded through me. The third line was rapidly moving up and down. Deciding that no body part could take the full impact, I pirouetted through it, distributing the searing agony.

I had made it.

On cotton legs, and with a spinning head, I stumbled out

of the labyrinth and collapsed onto the ground, lightheadedness overtaking me.

"Stay awake, stay awake, stay awake," I mumbled. "Find a safe place, then rest." My mind was strong, but my body won out. Unable to hold my lids open any longer, I tumbled into unconsciousness.

❧ 20 ❧

CLARA

W hen the blue archway shimmered into view, I took a deep breath, mentally preparing myself to enter the second magical kingdom, then said, "Let's hurry through before somebody decides to join us again."

Philip chortled. "I think our last few escapades might've scared off some of the princes."

"Only Simon. Felix seemed awfully persistent, and I wouldn't put it past Julian to show up as well." Only Leon hadn't found me, which filled my chest with irrational disappointment. I knew I had no right to hope he showed up when a big part of me didn't want him to, but my emotions didn't seem to care what was right and wrong.

Biscuit tapped the entrance with her horn, and the light grew stronger. As she jumped through the archway, I braced myself for the strange feeling that came with crossing from our world into a magical kingdom.

The spinning and whirling sensation wasn't too bad this time; however, my whole body was seized with an awful cold. I blinked snowflakes away from my eyelashes, staring in shock at my new surroundings. Since the first magic dimension had been the desert, I supposed it made sense for the second one to be the opposite. Still, it took me a minute to process that I had landed in a replica of Antarctica and that there was nothing but glaciers, snowcapped mountains, and ice as far as the eye could see.

"We better find whoever we came here to see before we freeze to death," I said, my words coming out as steam clouds from my mouth. When Philip didn't respond, I faced him, only to discover he wasn't there. "Philip? Philip!" I spun around. Nothing but snow and ice surrounded me. "We need to go back." I turned Biscuit around, making her go through the spot where the blue archway had been, but nothing happened. "Can't you do anything?" I touched her horn, but she shook her head, pushing my hand away. Perhaps that was the challenge of this kingdom. Perhaps I had to solve its mystery on my own while Philip waited for me back in the forest.

"Do you think it's going to be an animal again?" I shivered and wriggled my fingers and toes, hoping that would be enough to keep the circulation going. "All right. Let's do this before we get frostbite." I pushed Biscuit into a canter, surveying the white landscape. Would there be a cave again? Or some other landmark that hosted a magic elder? As if my thoughts had materialized it into being, a round igloo with a tunnel entrance appeared to my left. With no trees around it, I gave Biscuit a stern look after dismounting her. "Stay here. I'll be back soon." She neighed softly in response.

I kept my eyes on the ground as I walked toward the igloo. If I fell on ice, it would not only be much more painful than landing in a spider web but could also be deadly. Inside the igloo my breath caught at its lethal, natural beauty. Long icicles with sharp tips hung from the ceiling. The sole furniture was an ice throne, a white fox perched atop of it. Its fur was so clean and looked so soft, I wanted to reach out and run my fingers through it. Not that I would. Just because it looked sweet and gorgeous didn't mean it was harmless.

The fox winked at me. "Good, you're here. I was wondering when you would arrive."

"You knew I was coming?" Awkward silence followed when the fox didn't reply. "I'm here to complete a task in exchange for a gift that will help me succeed in the Inverse Kingdom."

The fox waved her paw, the human gesture looking surprisingly natural on her. "Sure, sure. But let's not talk about boring formalities, let's talk about the fun part. I like games. Do you like games?"

The memory of how the scorpion had almost made a meal out of me roused my apprehension, but I hid it behind a smile. "Of course. What kind of game?"

"Hide and seek. I'll hide, you seek. If you fail to find me by sundown, you lose and will give me your unicorn."

I balled my fists. The offer should have been less frightening than the one the scorpion had made since I got to keep my life, but the idea of being separated from Biscuit was too much to bear. Plus, I couldn't enter the Inverse Kingdom without her. I might not even be able to leave Antarctica without her help. But as scared as I was, I didn't dare to chicken out. I needed all the help I could get to fight the Mouse King. "What do I get if I win?"

"If you win, I will give you the power of the chameleon. Follow me." The fox didn't wait for me to agree. She jumped off her throne and darted out of the igloo and into the snow where she blended into the background. "Just as I can blend into the background here, so will you in the Inverse Kingdom. I'll tell you the magic words you must speak, but if you do get this gift, you must choose to use it wisely, for it has only a single use."

"I understand," I said, knowing that even though I

couldn't lose Biscuit, I had to take this gamble. What the fox offered could spell the difference between success and defeat, life and death in the Inverse Kingdom.

"You agree to the conditions?" The Fox's tail swept side to side in a mesmerizing pendulum-like motion.

"Yes, I do." The fox's coloring might blend into her snowy surroundings, but I was certain I could find her. However, as soon as the words left my mouth, my eyelids grew heavy, my limbs became weak, and I collapsed into the soft snow carpet. I didn't know how much time had passed when I regained consciousness. Standing up slowly, I shook off the snow sticking to my cloak. "What happened?"

Biscuit neighed softly but didn't do anything to indicate where the fox had disappeared to. The trickster must have put me to sleep. I looked up at the sky. The sun was low, close to the horizon. I had maybe one or two hours before sunset. An icy wind crashed into me, seeping through my clothes. Tears sprang to my eyes as the full extent of my situation hit me. I had to solve this riddle alone. If I failed, my journey would be over instantly. Without Biscuit, I wouldn't be able to leave this magical dimension, let alone enter the Inverse Kingdom and find the Crackatook. Unable to undo the curse, I would turn into a wooden doll. An ornament. I couldn't let that happen.

I mounted Biscuit and pushed her into a gallop. I would find the fox if I had to search this whole darn icy kingdom.

The snow-capped mountains didn't hide the fox, and neither did the frozen lake. Desperate, I got off Biscuit and dug through mounds of snow. My ruddy hands burned from the cold, and my nose ran. Still, I pressed on, using the igloo as my compass to ensure I wasn't walking in circles. When my fingers were too numb, I rubbed them, huffing warm air onto them. The wind howled, chilling me to my bone marrow, and snow fell from the sky, slowing my progress.

Everything blended together, and the sunlight grew weaker and weaker. When the sun was about to disappear behind the horizon, I had to admit the fox had won.

With chattering teeth and tears streaming down my face, I hurried over to Biscuit. "Thank you so much. I'm so sorry. I'll find a way to get you back. I promise." Biscuit brushed her snout against my cheek, wiping away the icicles from my cheeks. "I can't lose you. I can't," I sobbed, and that's when a thought occurred to me, snapping my head upright. I stared into Biscuit's dark-brown eyes. "This is crazy, but it's worth a try."

The fox had made me think she would hide in the snow because of her chameleon abilities, but what if she hid somewhere where there wasn't snow? Somewhere that I would dismiss as too easy.

My boots barely touched the ground as I raced the setting sun. It was only an inch away from being gone when I darted into the igloo where the fox was sitting lazily on her throne.

"I found you!" I pointed at her.

The fox's yellow eyes shone with annoyance, and she huffed, "Took you long enough."

Rude remarks came to my tongue, but I swallowed them, not wanting to infuriate the trickster.

"Well done. You passed the test. Sometimes the solutions are right in front of us, but we're too blind to see them." The fox pulled with her mouth two long white hairs from her tail and shot me an expectant gaze. I took the hairs from her.

"When you're ready to use the camouflage spell, eat the hairs and stand next to the spot you wish to blend into."

I raised my eyebrows. "But you said I would have to say a specific spell."

The fox shrugged. "If I didn't spread that rumor, anyone could come here and harass me, pulling hair out of my tail."

I nodded, understanding her need for self-preservation. "Thank you."

"You're welcome." The fox flicked her tail, and then she vanished behind her icy throne.

I mounted Biscuit and hoped the exit portal would not only return us to our world but also to Philip. My shoulder stiffened as the inside of my cloak chimed, and the nutcracker proclaimed, "Only six more days remain. If you don't solve the curse, you'll turn into a wooden doll and your soul will be locked for all eternity inside of me."

Half of my time was up. Only six days remained. If I failed to find the Crackatook, I would forever have to live with the knowledge that I had chosen to chase a hopeless quest instead of spending my last days with Father.

I swallowed hard, self-doubt sweeping over me. Was I foolish? Was there even a chance of me succeeding? Yes, there was. I had survived two magical kingdoms and gathered two magical trinkets. As long as I believed in myself, I would survive the next kingdom and make it into the Inverse Palace

A blue light shimmered in front of me, and Biscuit tapped it, transforming it into an archway. We galloped through it. I didn't mind the uncomfortable sensation, eager to see Philip. When we reemerged in the forest, I exhaled with relief as I met his worried green gaze.

"Clara!" Philip rushed toward me, and I slid off the saddle and into his arms. His lips pressed against mine without any hesitation. Unlike our first kiss that was slow and innocent, this one was demanding and passionate. His tongue circled mine, and his arms came around my waist. Despite the layers of clothing I wore, I felt every movement as if we were skin to skin. And yet, I wanted, needed more. I wanted to drink and breathe him in. I wanted to merge into one.

When Philip finally pulled away, I was no longer cold. Hot

tingles ran through my body, pooling in my abdomen, making me swell with giddiness and excitement.

"What was that?" I whispered to fill the silence.

"That was me showing you that I won't give up on you. Clara, I won't let you turn into a wooden doll. I'll fight for you, no matter what it takes."

The intensity in his voice scared me. It didn't matter how much we wanted to be together, we could never be. I was the crown princess of Austria and had responsibilities to my country and people.

Tears built behind my eyes, and I showed Philip the fox hair before I dissolved into sobs. "I got our second gift." My voice was wobbly, and my limbs trembled as the adrenaline abandoned me.

Philip's face fell, and I wanted to say that I would fight for him, that he meant so much to me it terrified me. Instead, I remained mum. I had no business making such promises. Even if we managed to break the curse and returned safely to Vienna, there was no way we could explore our romance. Father would never allow me to marry a guard, breaking mine and Philip's hearts. Looking at Philip now and seeing the tenderness in his eyes, I knew this wasn't a fleeting fancy. He was developing real feelings for me. I had to nip those feelings in the bud before any chances of us regaining our friendship became nil.

❧ 21 ❧

GRISELDA

A string quartet playing a waltz awoke me with a start. I pushed off the grass into a sitting position, trying to wipe away the remains of sleep and remember what had happened. The maze was behind me. Right, I had worked my way through it, and then I must've fallen asleep from exhaustion and the dizzying mist.

Rhythmical footsteps neared me. Two dozen ballerina dolls twirled and performed jetés, making their way over to me, their faces grim, ready to attack. They were as beautiful as Delilah and probably just as deadly. I jumped to my feet and rushed forward to the castle's entrance. I slipped through the heavy wooden-and-metal door and hurried down the marble corridor and up a dilapidated, uneven staircase. My feet pounded hard, but the staircase didn't grow shorter. It was as if the staircase created more and more stairs for me to conquer. The first line of ballerinas was so close to me now, I could hear the thudding noise of their pointe shoes. Desperate, I threw myself away from the staircase and onto the railing. As soon as my hands and legs hugged it, I shot upward. I screamed, fear rippling through me as my brain tried to comprehend that this was another inverse aspect of this strange place.

At the top, my hammering heart skipped a beat. There was about a foot of floor in front of me, a tall column on each side, but beyond that there was no floor. A huge chunk of the corridor, which would connect me to the rooms on the second floor was missing, revealing an eighteen-foot fall and the first floor underneath. The only thing connecting the two parts of the second floor was a rope wrapped tightly around a marble column on each side. Underneath the rope, the ballerinas were lined up, stretching their arms upward to catch my body if I fell. Their teeth snapped, and their eyes shone with darkness, making me certain falling to my death would be preferable than being at their mercy.

Since I could neither stay here forever, nor go down the staircase, I had to use the rope and somehow balance to the other side. How I wished I could shift into a tiny mouse, instead of staying in my half-mouse, half-human form. I closed my eyes and focused hard, but as I had suspected a transformation was impossible. Telling myself that my tail and whiskers wouldn't let me fall, I gingerly put one foot on the rope, then the other. I repeated the action, mumbling, "One step at a time."

The classical music flared up so loud my eardrums were ready to rupture. Through the sensation of my skull splitting in two and my heart racing, I continued across the rope. When I had only three feet left, I felt pressure being applied to the rope behind me. Not turning around to see what was going on out of fear of losing my balance, I pressed on. And then it happened, the cord collapsed. I shifted my weight forward and managed to grab onto the sharp edges of the floor. Using arm strength I didn't know I possessed, I pulled myself up onto the ground. Behind me a ballerina with scissors scowled. My body broke out in an uncontrollable tremble. I sat like that for a while until my breaths grew even. I had made it. I was still alive.

I rose and crept down the corridor toward the big metal door at the end. The brass door knocker, a mouse with narrowed eyes and sharp teeth holding a big ring in its mouth, made shivers run down my legs. Ignoring it, I shoved the door handle down. The door creaked open, and I stepped through into a large room with high ceilings and tall windows where toy soldiers marched up and down, heavy shotguns slung across their shoulders.

I was certain the Mouse King was behind this room and that me crossing it was the next challenge. The open design and the light streaming through the tall windows made it impossible for me to remain undetected. I strode forward and prayed the soldiers didn't choose to attack me. My walk was confident but not so confident as to appear threatening. Almost halfway through the room, a general jumped into my path, and I found myself staring at the hollow end of his long rifle.

"What is your business here?"

"I'm here to see the seven-headed Mouse King."

He pushed the gun's tip into my chest. "Have you come to assassinate him?"

"No, I have come to ask him for help," I managed past the stone lodged in my throat.

The soldier motioned with his hand, and two new soldiers stepped in, each grabbing one of my arms. "Escort her to the Mouse King. See what he wants to do with her."

The soldiers saluted and marched me out of the room. Nerves seized me. What if the Mouse King refused to help me? What if he blamed me for Clara coming here? What if he gave the soldiers the order to execute me?

The room I was escorted into didn't ease my worries. The space was bathed in darkness, illuminated only by skinny rays of sunlight streaming through the small, smudged windows. Judging by how much my footsteps echoed, I assumed it was as vast as the previous room, but I couldn't tell for sure since I couldn't see how far it extended. What I could tell, even despite the lack of light, was that this space was in a severely decrepit state, the floor uneven, the walls peeling, with an icky, moldy smell hanging heavy in the air.

"You have a visitor, my king," one of the soldiers said and gave my back a hard shove, making me almost stumble and fall on my face.

Out of the shadows, a hunched figure stepped forward. An involuntary gasp escaped me. Even though I had known the Mouse King would have seven heads, that didn't diminish the disturbing sight of them. Seven necks moved like cobras, bringing the heads forward for seven pairs of red eyes to scrutinize me.

Just like me, the king was a mixture between a mouse and a human. He was about my height, but much wider. His hind legs were bent, his ears weren't quite round, and his tail almost reached the ground. A grotesque creature, he made me want to shrink back. My fear of what he would do to me if he noticed my disgust made me keep a neutral facial expression. For the first time, I wondered how others saw me. Was I hideous? Was my ability to shift between a human and a mouse unnatural, as everyone said? Had Clara and the emperor been justified in banishing me to Snake Island?

"Who are you? How dare you break into my palace?" the Mouse King hissed. A snake slithered past him and toward me, and I froze certain that I was one wrong word or move away from being bitten. "If you expect mercy for being a mouse shifter, I have bad news for you. I don't welcome intruders, no matter what they are."

My stomach tightened, sweat broke out on my forehead, and my fingers trembled. Why had I thought it was a good idea to come to the Mouse King? Why hadn't I gone somewhere new and started afresh after my Snake Island escape? Why had I been so hell-bent on destroying Clara and the emperor? Was that truly my goal, something that I wanted to do? Or was I acting out my mother's legacy? Was I following her dreams of becoming an empress, confined by her expectations?

"Are you mute?" The Mouse King advanced on me, and I clutched my hands tightly behind my back to stop them from fidgeting.

"I am here to request your help. My mother was executed for being a mouse shifter, and I have been imprisoned for the last ten years for shifting in front of my stepsister. Princess Clara and the emperor of Austria are responsible for both atrocities, and I seek revenge against them."

The Mouse King shrugged, making his seven heads move up and down, while his snake slithered around me. "Why should I care? Do you think I would ever be successful, have all of this—" He motioned at the dilapidated room around himself. "—if I wasted my time helping every creature that came to me?"

"I'm—"

"You think you're special, that we're kin just because we are mouse shifters," he interrupted. "Well, I have news for you. I don't need an alliance with a mouse shifter, so I have no reason to help you. In fact, I'm feeling inclined to execute you just because I can." The snake raised its head, growing to the size of a dragon, and its red, forked tongue shot out.

I transformed my panic into determination and said tartly, "You will not execute me if you want to keep your kingdom and your life. Clara of Austria is coming here to destroy you."

All seven pairs of eyes narrowed, and the snake shrank a bit. "If you're lying, your death will be very painful."

"Clara is coming here to steal the Crackatook and end

you. She's the girl from the prophecy. She will be your undoing."

His whiskers twitched, and his tail swung back and forth. His snake reverted to its original size and hid behind him.

My shoulders dropped an inch. I could focus his rage on Clara. "If you give me what I want, I'll make sure she fails."

The Mouse King snorted. "I don't need a girl helping me defeat another girl."

"She won't be alone. She's coming with a unicorn and magic." I wasn't 100 percent certain about the unicorn and the magic, but knew I had to be prepared for everything, and that the Mouse King would only help me if he truly believed Clara was his foretold destroyer.

My words had the intended effect, making the Mouse King pace.

"If you kill me, you're risking your own life. But if you help me, we can ensure that it's Clara who dies."

Seven pairs of lips thinned into seven hard lines. "How do I know you speak the truth and that you aren't working with this Clara?"

"Her father had my mother executed. He banished me to Snake Island to live out my life in a prison." I hung on to my hate and anger, a never-ending well of energy, reminding myself that any other emotions were weaknesses. So what if I was living out my mother's wish to become an empress, who cared? Her wish had propelled me forward. If not for having a goal, I would still be in Snake Island, rotting away. My rage had brought me here. It would ensure that I reclaimed my social standing and became the empress I was meant to be.

The Mouse King produced a dagger, and I planted my feet into the floor to stop myself from inching backward as he grabbed my hand and sliced a finger. He did the same to his index finger and pressed it against mine. "Our deal is sealed in blood. We will work together to bring down Princess Clara."

"And put me on throne of Austria," I added.

"Yes." He flashed his sharp teeth, injecting fear into the excitement running through my veins.

❧ 22 ❧

CLARA

As Philip and I rode through the thick forest, I filled him in on everything that happened in the Antarctica realm.

"You solved the riddle and received the chameleon gift... but you seem down," Philip said.

I glared at him. "You think? Would you be happy if you had only six more days to solve a curse before you turn into a wooden doll?" My deflection seemed to work because he fell silent once again, and I went back to ignoring him, something I had done ever since our second kiss. While Philip thought I was sulking, I tried coming up with a way to make it clear to him that whatever was between us could never work due to what was expected of me as the heir of Austria. I had disappointed Father enough. My carelessness had led me to touch the nutcracker and unleash the curse. If I survived this journey and broke the curse, I would do better. I would become the princess Austria deserved and the daughter Father needed.

As logical as my reasoning was, I couldn't share it with Philip. He would fight for me, for us, and make it that much harder for me to fulfil my duties. Thus, I had to make him believe I didn't want to be with him.

He reached over to take my hand, but I pulled away.

"What's wrong, Clara? Please talk to me." Concern shone in his green eyes, and I quickly looked away before I turned weak.

Gathering my resolve, I sat straight up. "The kiss—I mean the kisses," I corrected myself, "were mistakes. That can't happen again."

"Why? I don't think they were mistakes. I wanted to kiss you, and you wanted to kiss me, didn't you?" His forehead creased, and I was tempted to lie and say I never had wanted to kiss him in the first place. But that was too much of an untruth, one I couldn't pull off convincingly, so I resorted to the next best thing.

"I thought I wanted to kiss you, but I know now that I was merely curious. I wanted to experience what it felt like to be kissed." I gave him a tight-lipped smile. "I felt safe with you, Philip, so I thought it would make sense to kiss you. And now that I did, I realize I only have friendly feelings for you, nothing more."

His face fell, and a blade wrenched into my chest.

"It didn't feel like exploration or curiosity," he said after a long pause.

"I'm sorry if I gave you the wrong impression."

"Is this because your father wants you to marry one of the four princes? Are you afraid of him? Because I'm not."

I tilted my chin up and emphasized every word. "This has nothing to do with my father. I simply don't have romantic feelings for you. The quicker you accept that, the better for everyone." When a blue light shimmered in front of me, I guided Biscuit without any hesitation toward it. Entering the third magical dimension and completing a potentially deadly quest was preferable to my uncomfortable conversation with Philip.

With a tap of her horn, Biscuit transformed the light into an archway, and we galloped into the realm.

The colors disintegrated, my ears rang, and I prepared myself for the worst, wondering what brutal conditions awaited us in the third kingdom. Would it be as hot as the first and full of poisonous creatures? Or would it be as icy as the second with a trickster host?

As my body adjusted to the new realm, however, I didn't feel any discomfort. The air was balmy, the sun shone brightly, but not painfully, and the noise of waves breaking against the shore filled my ears. I had landed in a paradise filled with palm trees, the ocean, and cute one story, multi-colored houses. The place looked like one of the Caribbean islands depicted in my geography books. I had never thought I would ever see anything like it, and deep gratitude filled me.

My gaze went skyward, searching for clouds to indicate we were about to be struck by a hurricane or other natural disaster since this moderate climate was too good to be true. The azure sky with not a single cloud in sight eased my worries. The streets too seemed safe. No danger was lurking, no tigers or other wild animals were coming our way. And what was up with all the houses? Did this realm have people? Was I finally going to negotiate with a human being, perhaps even one who wanted to help me, not deliver me to a torturous death or take something from me?

"This is amazing," Philip said next to me, mirroring my thoughts. "I wish I could stay here forever."

I pointed at a pink-colored mansion across the street that read Hotel Paradise. "We should go there and ask for directions."

Philip gave a rigid nod, and I smiled, calmness and happiness flowing through me. We'd only arrived in this kingdom, but I already knew our stay here would be wonderful.

We bound Biscuit and Ace outside the hotel, who tilted their head serenely, and strode inside where two beautiful women awaited us at the reception, each wearing a pink hibiscus flower in their silky hair.

"Welcome to Hotel Paradise. Please allow us to take care of you," they said in unison, and the woman on the right motioned for me to step forward, while the one on the left tended to Philip.

"Would you like to start with a milk-and-honey bath?" the one on the right asked.

I blinked. I'd been pampered at Schönbrunn palace and had enjoyed it a lot, but that's not why I was here. I was running out of time to find the Crackatook. And even if I wasn't, I probably didn't carry enough gold on me to pay for beauty treatments.

"I'll sign you up for the whole spa package," the woman continued, taking my pause for indecisiveness. "You'll love it. It's really soothing."

"But...." I squeezed the space between my brows, trying to remember the rest of my objection. When I couldn't, I focused on why I was here. Right, the Crackatook. "We're on our way to the Inverse Kingdom, and we have come to seek help from your magic elder," I said, hoping my honesty wouldn't get us into trouble.

"Yes, of course," the woman replied with a friendly smile. "I will pass on your message, but until then, please enjoy our amenities. We're always happy to have guests."

Before I could protest, she whisked me away toward the staircase on the right as Philip was guided away to the staircase on the left.

I halted. "Where is my companion going? Can't he come with us?"

She shook her head. "I'm taking you to the ladies' room. He's going to the gentlemen's room to receive his personalized treatment."

"Right." My cheeks heated at my stupidity. Not allowing myself to imagine Philip's body being pampered in a claw-foot bath, I quickly switched the topic. "How long will it take for you to pass on my message?"

"I'll make sure he gets it as soon as possible." She opened a door to a bathroom where a tub filled with milky water and rose petals stood. "Please take a soak before the masseuse arrives."

I did, basking in the first proper bath I had in a week, the warm water and softness of the milk and honey soothing me.

After a while, another woman came for me and handed me a bathrobe. "Please follow me." She took me into a room filled with candles, a calming melody playing from a music box, and a massage table. "Please undress and put your head in the opening."

She exited, and I put the bathrobe onto a chair in the corner where my other clothes were already lying. As I got comfortable underneath the sheet on the bed, a chime sounded and then the nutcracker's gravelly voice said, "Only five more days remain. If you don't solve the curse, you'll turn into a wooden doll and your soul will be locked for all eternity inside of me."

I waved my hand impatiently at him, willing him to shut up. When he did, I exhaled and focused on the sweet notes coming from the music box.

There was a knock, and then a pair of black, low-heeled shoes came toward me. "Hello, Clara, I will be doing your massage today."

"How did you know my name?" was on my tongue, but the question disintegrated as small, yet strong hands rubbed my back. Almond oil was put on my skin, and the masseuse worked out knots I hadn't known I had. After all the strenuous riding, the pampering was heavenly. All my concerns lifted from my mind, and I relaxed completely, enjoying the moment instead of agonizing about the future. Why had I been so worried about the future anyway? The longer I lay on the bed, enjoying my massage, the harder it was to remember why I had been so distressed. Was I simply a worrywart, prone to overreacting?

After every inch of my body had turned into a blissful gooey mess, including my scalp and soles, the masseuse moved on to my face.

"How does a pumpkin and apricot mask sound?"

"Delicious," I murmured, not bothering to open my eyes.

She put a bowl with steaming water in front of my face to open my pores, then applied a cooling mixture, which my dry skin inhaled with vigor.

"Now, I want you to rest. Simply ring the bell when you wake up."

I wanted to reply something, but my lips felt too heavy, my tongue too thick. Sleep pulled me under, and I was only too glad to let it, basking in finally having a bed once again.

When I awoke, I had no idea how long I had slept. A wave of panic and guilt encased me. I didn't know exactly why what I was doing was wrong, only that it was. I sprang off the bed and rang the bell, quickly pulling on my bathrobe since my riding dress and undergarments were gone.

A maid entered, and I demanded, "Where are my clothes?"

"We put them in your bedroom. We washed your dress and undergarments."

"Thank you." I softened my tone, feeling silly at my outburst.

"Of course. Please let me show you your chamber. It has a full wardrobe." The maid walked me into a bedroom that rivaled mine back home. The bed was a four-poster and large enough to accommodate three people, and the closet held anything one could desire. I breathed a sigh of relief as I found my coat and felt the invisible purse through the inside pocket. Good, the nutcracker and the vials were still there. Why were they so important again?

"Please pick a dress for dinner." The maid interrupted my thoughts.

Surveying the expensive garments, I shook my head. "I can't. It's too much."

Ignoring my remark, the maid pulled out a lovely lavender gown from the closet. "You would look stunning in this. And these shoes would go perfectly with it." She produced lilac heels adorned with tiny flowers. "We could leave your hair down for a youthful look. After your treatments, you don't even need makeup."

The shoes and the dress were too much to resist, so I nodded. "It's a bit too fancy for a dinner though," I said weakly, itching to slip into my new outfit.

"But it's not just any dinner. The queen's nephew has agreed to see you."

I tried to process this information, my brain working sluggishly, as if underwater. "You have a queen?"

The masseuse nodded eagerly. "Her nephew will dine with you."

"Will he be able to tell me how to navigate the Inverse Kingdom?"

The masseuse nodded. "Yes, of course."

Something about her cheerful tone rubbed me the wrong way, but I couldn't put my finger on what it was exactly. The notion was so fleeting, I decided not to pay it any attention. I was overreacting. What I needed to do was put on the beautiful dress and shoes and ensure I had a wonderful dinner. I deserved it.

The dress hugged every curve of my body without being too snug, the material light and flowy. Although the shoes had a high heel, they were comfortable, and I floated down the staircase. The dining room glistened with chandeliers and candlelight. Notes of coriander, rosemary, and lemon filled the air. Delicious-looking dishes of meat, fish, and desserts lined the tables, making me salivate after a week of mostly eating bread. But it wasn't the décor or the food that mesmerized me, but the face that stared at me from across the long table.

"It is you," I breathed.

❧ 23 ❧

CLARA

"I've missed you," Prince Leon said, and I glided toward him. His shoulder-length mane of blond hair shone like spun gold, his eyes were an intense cerulean, and his face was that of a Greek god—strong chin, nose and high forehead.

He placed my hand on top of his and guided me to a seat next to him.

The waiter popped a golden bottle of champagne with an intricate label depicting swans. He poured two glasses, and tiny pearls bubbled to the surface.

"Did you enjoy your treatments today?" Leon tilted his head, his gaze pulling me in, captivating me.

"Yes, it was wonderful." My voice had a fluffy, translucent quality to it, and my brain was made from cotton or a cloud, perhaps both, a cotton cloud. The thought made me giggle, and I took a sip from my flute to clear my thoughts. But the bubbly deliciousness only muddled my mind further. Vaguely, I remembered there was something that had brought me here —a reason, a purpose. I pondered this as I bit into my smoked salmon wrapped in seaweed appetizer, and then it came to me. I had been on a journey. Why I had been on one

I couldn't recall, but I did remember that I hadn't been alone. "Where's Philip?"

Leon's face contorted for a split second, but then he gave me the most dazzling smile. "He wanted to take his dinner in his room after his treatments. He was so relaxed, he didn't feel like dressing up and coming down."

I nodded. That made sense since I had fallen asleep after my own treatment. Still, something continued to bother me. "I'm happy to see you, but I don't understand what you're doing here." I motioned around the grand room, realizing that in a way it made perfect sense for striking Leon to be surrounded by this much beauty and extravagance.

"I'm Queen Bev's nephew. I often stay here. We're very close." Leon refilled my flute even though it was only half empty.

"How nice." I rubbed my temple, trying and failing to connect the two pieces of information and figure out what it meant that Leon was the nephew of the queen. It was only when my entrée of pork chops and roasted potatoes with truffles arrived that I made the connection. "If you are the queen's nephew, that means you have magic in your blood."

Leon intertwined his fingers with mine. "That's right. It also means I can share with you the best hidden places of this paradise." He winked, and I giggled, flattered by his attention.

A dull voice in the back of my head was warning me, screaming that magic meant danger. But the voice was so quiet, so far away, it was easy to shush it and focus on Leon. "What places?"

"Let that be a surprise. I'll show you after dessert."

Dessert was a delicious, fluffy tiramisu with a rum-soaked base. The combination of the rum and the champagne made my head spin. When I stood up, I careened and bumped into the table. Thankfully, Leon's strong hands were there to hold me up.

"Let me show you what I call the view." He pulled me up a purple carpeted staircase, then pushed open a gilded glass door, which led to the balcony. I inhaled the fresh ocean air. The moon illuminated the endless inky water as waves broke in a soothing rhythm against the shore.

Leon and I talked about different topics, the conversation constantly flowing, but nothing we talked about stayed in my head for too long, which had transformed into a sieve. I only remembered that I laughed a lot and complimented Leon on his great qualities, which included his bravery, kindness, and excellent taste. When he leaned forward to kiss me, I flinched back. Embarrassed by my strange reaction, I stammered, "I'm sorry." I bit my lip. What was wrong with me? Why didn't I want this perfect man to kiss me after a perfect evening?

"Did I come on too strong?" The disappointment on Leon's face broke me, and I hurried to come up with a good reason for my odd behavior.

"I need to spend a bit more time with you before we take this any further." I bunched up and straightened my skirt. "It's getting late. I think it would be best if I go to bed now."

Leon smiled and took my hand. "Of course. Let me walk you to your room." At my door, he pressed a kiss to my hand and left, always the perfect nobleman.

As soon as I slipped off my shoes and dress, I tumbled into bed, my eyes drooping shut. I fell asleep to a rattling noise and a mechanic voice. "Only four more days remain. If you don't solve the curse, you'll turn into a wooden doll and your soul will be locked for all eternity inside of me."

The next day, Leon took me out onto the ocean in a white catamaran. We watched dolphins frolic in the water, sipped Bellinis, and noshed on strawberries and finger sandwiches.

The boat stayed close to the shore, and Leon pointed out all the attractions and important buildings. When we were passing a grotto, I asked, "What's that?"

"Nothing. Just a cave." Leon's voice was strained, as if he was angry, but when I studied his face, he was smiling. He lifted my hand and twirled me, slow dancing to the music the violinist played on board.

I relaxed into Leon's arms, listening to the sweet melody and trying to keep up with his smooth movements. Why had the cave seemed so important? I had no idea, and after a while, I decided to forget about it.

We stayed on the catamaran for dinner. As soon as the sun set, dread overcame me. Would Leon try to kiss me? Why was I so afraid of him kissing me? Did everyone experience this type of nerves, or was I silly, making myself crazy?

To my relief and disappointment, Leon didn't attempt to kiss me. When the catamaran reached the docks, he took my hands in his and gazed deeply into my eyes. "I think you're right about the kissing. We should wait until you're ready."

My heart warmed at his sweetness and understanding.

"Especially since we have a whole lifetime ahead of us."

I squinted, unsure what he was saying.

"Clara, I'm falling in love with you. I want you to become my fiancée."

"You want us to get engaged?" My lips trembled.

"Yes. Tomorrow I'm going to ask you to become my wife. I didn't want to blindside you, so I'm giving you one day to think about it."

He pulled out a beautiful ring with a round-cut diamond that was the biggest gemstone I had ever seen. "Nothing would make me happier than putting this on your hand and spending the rest of my life with you."

I stared from the magnificent ring into Leon's azure eyes. How could I say no to him? He was perfect. This was perfect.

I leaned into him and his arm came around my waist, pulling me into a sideways hug. We stayed like that, only disentangling when the catamaran reached the shore. Like the previous night, Leon walked me to my room. Knowing he would propose to me tomorrow made me feel weightless like a balloon ready to soar into the sky. Or did it? Behind the exhilaration, something was telling me that this was all wrong. I shook my head, but the confusions stayed with me. I didn't know which part of me could I trust.

It was hard to say goodnight to Leon. I didn't want to be alone. I didn't know what to do with the ache that spread in my chest as I lay in bed. To cheer myself up, I hummed one of the melodies I had heard earlier on the ship and drowned out the muttering coming from my cloak in the corner.

"Only three more days remain. If you don't solve the curse, you'll turn into a wooden doll and your soul will be locked for all eternity inside of me."

A knock on the door tore me out of my reverie. I darted over, hoping Leon had returned, unable to say goodbye for the night. But instead of blond hair and blue eyes, it was green eyes and dark hair that greeted me. The face didn't look happy or serene as Leon's did; it was tense and pale. The clothes of the man in front of me were dirty and streaked with blood, and I struggled for a moment to place him.

"Clara," he said with a note of longing in his voice, and several images flooded my mind. Me and the stranger laughing. Us horseback riding. Us walking through an enchanted village. Us weathering the desert.

"Philip." I blinked rapidly, trying to connect the thoughts that were moving too fast for me to catch.

He pushed past me into the room and locked the door. "What have they done to you?"

"Nothing." I examined his sorry state. "What happened to you?"

"I was thrown into the dungeons. Again. I really don't want it to become a habit. I escaped and searched everywhere for you. I was worried about you, but clearly, I shouldn't have been." He crossed his arms, as if waiting for an explanation.

"I'm fine." At his incredulous look, I added, "I'm sure it was a misunderstanding that you were locked up. An oversight."

"A misunderstanding? An oversight?" Philip grabbed my shoulders and shook me. "Clara, wake up!"

Footsteps neared my door and what I recognized as the maid's voice floated through the wall, "Is everything all right, Princess Clara?"

"Yes, everything's swell. I was just replaying my wonderful evening with Prince Leon."

"You two make such a gorgeous couple."

"Thank you. I'm going to bed now."

"Good night. Have a restful sleep!"

I turned to Philip and hissed, "You need to go."

He cocked his head. "Why? If you really believe I was locked up by accident, there's no need for me to hide."

His reasoning made sense, but on a gut level I knew he wasn't safe. A dull ache started at the back of my head. "I'm sorry, I can't deal with this right now. It's too much." He opened his mouth to protest, but I cut him off. "If you say another word, I'm going to call the maid. I need time to process this." I waved my hands around wildly. "All of this."

Philip inhaled deeply. "Fine. But you better not take too much time unless you want to turn into a wooden doll. Also, I've made my prison cell look like someone is sleeping in the cot, but a guard checks on me every night. I need to be gone by tomorrow night."

He slipped out of the room, leaving me to wonder how he knew the phrase the nutcracker kept telling me. I took out the figurine and studied it. Had I shared this weird toy with Philip? And could what it was saying really become reality?

With my headache reaching an intense throbbing, I took the glass of water left for me on my bedside table and emptied it in a few gulps. Immediately, my muscles relaxed, my thoughts ceased, and I was knocked out into a deep sleep.

❧ 24 ❧

CLARA

I woke up with dry eyes and a stiff neck, and an ominous feeling. Something was wrong. I glanced at the empty water glass on my bedside table. I remembered drinking it and passing out immediately. Sure, I had been tired, but the depth of my sleep seemed unnatural. I sniffed the glass. It smelled sweet, not the way water should. Massaging my shoulders, Philip's stern talk came to me in bits and pieces, and then the events of the previous night assaulted me like a wrecking ball.

Philip trying to make me understand, me sending him away. I had drooled over Leon who I didn't even know, and who clearly had ordered the maid to give me a sleeping draught. What other substances had he given me? If my rapid falling asleep had been induced, were my feelings for him induced too?

As if my morning wasn't awful enough, the nutcracker chimed, "Only two more days remain. If you don't solve the curse, you'll turn into a wooden doll and your soul will be locked for all eternity inside of me."

How was that possible? I had entered the third magical

kingdom with five days left and was already down to two. Tears of desperation, anger, and betrayal rushed into my eyes. It would have been so easy to dissolve and cry over the precious time I had lost. But I refused to play the victim. Leon tricking me stung and made me feel foolish. I hated him and myself. But just because he had won the last round didn't mean I would give up. Philip was somewhere out there, and as soon as I found him, I would leave this phony place.

A knock came from the door, and my maid entered with a breakfast tray, which held orange juice, croissants, omelet, and fruit. "Prince Leon is very busy with the preparations for the engagement, so he won't be able to join you for breakfast or lunch."

I put on my most innocent smile and replied, "I totally understand." Leaning forward, I added dreamily, "I can't wait to see what he has planned for me." I picked up the brochure with different spa treatments from the bedside table and pointed to the lengthiest. "I want to look my best for my engagement. Could you book me in for a mud bath and a sugar scrub exfoliation?" Together the treatments should take three hours, plenty of time to escape the hotel.

"Of course. When would you like to do it?"

"Right after breakfast."

The maid nodded with approval and pushed the tray at me. "But first you must eat your breakfast."

I picked up my fork and stuffed a big chunk of the omelet into my mouth, chewing with gusto.

Satisfied, the maid exited, calling, "I'll send the masseuse right over."

As soon as the door locked, I spat out the omelet and stuffed all the food items into the back of the closet. I threw on the most practical dress in my wardrobe, a thin suede number roomy enough for horseback riding, pulled on the only non-heeled shoes, and checked my cloak, which still held the invisible bag with the nutcracker and two vials.

Hiding behind the door, I waited.

"Princess Clara?" a voice trilled through the wall a few minutes later.

"Come in."

The door swung open, the masseuse entered, and I hit her full force with the tray. She staggered, and I smacked her again for good measure. Her knees gave out, and I captured her shoulders, lowering her carefully to the ground. "I'm sorry, but this had to be done." I pulled her into my closet, not wanting her to be discovered in case the maid decided to tidy up my room. As another security measure, I bound the masseuse's wrists and ankles together with dresses and stuffed a shawl into her mouth to keep her from screaming when she woke up.

Then I slipped out of the room and down the corridor. With my head clear, it wasn't too hard to avoid the servants going through the Paradise Hotel. Was it even a hotel? For all I knew, this was an old dilapidated house, only appearing beautiful due to the magic cast over it. I would probably never find out, and it didn't matter. I had to flee this sham of a place. I continued down a staircase and pushed open the first door. Too late did I realize it led into the gardens and not the street.

I scrambled to figure out a way to find Philip when a waitress floated through the garden toward me. Quickly, I ducked behind a large rosebush. My nose tingled at the smell coming from the glasses on the waitress's tray, and my hand twitched, eager to reach out and grab one of the beverages.

I held my hand still with my other and breathed a sigh of relief as the waitress left. Whatever tonic I had been given in this kingdom was no joke. I had developed a dependency toward it and would have to wean myself off it.

Alone again, I continued my way through the garden, hoping to either discover Philip or an exit. Halfway through, a familiar whistling reached my ears.

I turned around and was met by an intense green gaze. "Are you ready to hear me out now?" Philip asked.

I nodded, and when I spoke, my voice was choked. "I was under Leon's spell. I don't know if he actually put a spell on me, but there was something in my drinks to make me fall asleep and probably to make me relaxed and happy."

Anger, fear, and pain flashed across Philip's face. He took my hands. "It's over now. We need to leave."

"Yes, but first we need to find the trinket we came here for."

Philip shook his head. "Leon will never allow us to do that."

"I think he will." I petted my hidden purse. "Leon didn't talk to me once about the nutcracker or what we were doing in the magical kingdoms. I don't think he's too concerned with the spell as long as I marry him. I informally agreed to an engagement yesterday, and our official engagement will be today. He thinks he already won." I swallowed hard, aching at the words I had to speak. "He wants the kingdom, and he'll get it if he marries me before I turn into a wooden doll. He doesn't care what happens to me as long as he becomes king."

"I'm sorry," Philip whispered, then added, "Even if Leon's not worried, he will still have some guards around wherever the trinket is. We can't walk around this island searching for it. We don't have time." He glanced over my shoulder. "It will take Leon a few hours at most to realize you're missing."

I smiled up at Philip. "But I do know where the trinket is. Leon took me out on a boat, and we sailed past a cave. I'm certain that's where we're going to find the third charm."

Philip still didn't look convinced, but said, "You think you can find the cave?" I nodded. "All right. What about Biscuit and Ace?"

"We can't leave them behind." I thought for a moment. "We'll get them first, bring them on the ship, and then we find a way off this island through the cave."

Philip tugged a hand roughly through his hair. "Why do you think the portal is at this cave?"

"Because everything about that area felt different. I've traveled through several portals, and they all had a strong energy like the grotto. Even if there's the slightest chance of a portal, we need to bring Biscuit, so we can leave this island as soon as possible."

"Now that we can agree on." The corners of his lips tugged upward in the most adorable way, making me want to kiss every inch of his mouth and reminding me that even if we solved the nutcracker curse, my heart would still be broken.

❧ 25 ❧

CLARA

Unlike the last time, when it had been relatively easy to steal the horses from an empty barn, I discovered that Leon's people were no amateurs. Biscuit and Ace had two attendants each. Since an ambush would land us in prison, we tiptoed out of the barn before the attendants could see us and hid behind a fence to figure out a plan. It was then that something bothersome occurred to me. I turned to Philip and whispered, "What if the guards check on you before evening? They'll put two and two together."

Philip smirked. "I made it look as if I drowned." He pointed at his clothes. "I stole these. My personal clothes are in the ocean and the window of my cell is smashed in. It was directly above the ocean."

"Is that how you escaped?"

Philip shrugged nonchalantly, but I could see the worry line between his brows. "Yes, I jumped out of the window and into the ocean."

"Did it hurt?" Alone thinking about the high drop made goose bumps break out on my body. And then there was the vast ocean. Even though I had been in a haze on my catamaran excursion with Leon, I remembered the water looking extra shiny and sparkly, beautiful on the surface, dangerous underneath. Who knew what creatures were hidden in its depths?

Philip rubbed his arm. "It wasn't pleasant, but I survived, and I didn't break anything."

"I'm glad you did." My cheeks heated, and I remembered I was supposed to act cold, snuff out any foolish hopes Philip had about us being together. "It's good to know that if we fall into the water, nothing bad will happen."

Philip's gaze traveled to my mouth for a second before it returned to my eyes, and he inclined his head toward the barn, which was surrounded by a stone wall. "One of us needs to distract the guards while the other steals the horses. If they see you, we're done. I'll distract them."

"All right." I wasn't nervous about freeing the horses, but I was nervous about what the attendants would do to Philip. Did they have swords? Daggers? Magic? "Please be safe." I stared deep into his eyes, unable to hide my feelings for him.

"I will." His lips brushed against mine softly, and I melted into his chest despite knowing better. When he pulled away, he didn't say anything, simply guided me toward the barn. He intertwined his hands, and I put my foot into them. He helped me up the stone wall surrounding the barn. Right above Biscuit and Ace, I stayed completely quiet and begged the heaven that the attendants wouldn't look up.

A loud whistle came, and the four attendees exchanged glances.

"What was that?" one asked.

"We should check it out," another said and left together with the first one. Two attendants remained. A scream pierced the air, and the third attendant ran toward it. The last one remained, but I couldn't wait any longer, afraid the scream would arouse nearby guards, and even alert Leon.

I jumped down from the wall on top of the shoulders of the attendant. My weight shoved him forward, and he staggered, then fell onto his knees. His sword clanked to the ground, and I grabbed the cool steel, using the heel to knock him out. When he didn't move, I hurried to Biscuit and Ace, released their reins, and jumped on Biscuit's back with Ace following us.

Outside the barn, one guard was down, blood oozing from his chest while Philip fought the other two guards. Despite his skill, he was struggling in this unfair match. He managed to disarm one of the guards and shove him to the ground. But then the other drove his sword into Philip's side, and he swayed, blood trickling from his stomach.

My breath hitched, and I froze before realizing I couldn't just stand around. I had to do something. Grabbing the white vial the scorpion had given me, I sprinkled one drop each on the guards. Immediately, they froze.

"Get on Ace, let's go," I yelled at Philip who remained on the floor, as if he too was paralyzed.

I didn't need to tell him twice. He crawled onto his stallion, and I winced at his suppressed moan of pain. Tending to Philip's wound would have to wait. First, we needed to leave the scene of the crime and find a boat.

We galloped to the marina where a medium-sized sailboat caught my attention. Two guards were walking up and down the promenade, and I was certain more were nearby, waiting for an alarm to sound.

"We need to come back in the evening," I said with resignation, the adrenaline leaving my veins.

"No," Philip protested in a firm voice. "If we do that, we might miss our window of opportunity. I can take them."

The determination on his face told me he would stop the guards with any means necessary, including more injuries to himself. But this was my mission, not Philip's, and I wouldn't watch him be hurt any further. For the second time that day, I pulled out the paralyzation potion.

"What are you doing?" Philip asked as I pushed Biscuit into a gallop.

The guards swiveled around at the sound of hooves nearing, but it was too late. I sprinkled the last two drops of the white vial on them. They froze, and I hurried toward the sailboat where Philip was already maneuvering the ropes. I joined him and calmed the horses, who didn't seem too eager to travel by water.

Philip worked without saying a word. It was only when we were far from shore, the island growing smaller and smaller that he turned on me. "How could you use up all of the paralyzation potion?"

"I had no choice."

"We needed it to defeat the Mouse King."

"We needed it now." With each sentence, our voices grew louder and louder.

"Why did you do it?" Accusation flashed in Philip's face.

"Because I can't watch you bleed out." I tore off a piece from my sleeve to wrap it around his wound. "Does it need to be cleaned?"

Philip lifted his linen shirt, and I made myself look at the mostly coagulated wound and shredded skin.

"I think it's fine; there's no dirt. Plus, I doubt there's anything on this boat to disinfect it with."

"I'll have a look." Not waiting for his answer, I rushed off. Relief relaxed my muscles when I spotted a half empty vodka bottle.

Returning to Philip, I commanded, "Lie down," as if I had done this many times before.

To my surprise, he obeyed, not making a fuss. I uncorked the bottle and poured the clear liquid over his wound. Even though barely a sound escaped his lips, I could see from the contorting of his face that he was in great pain. And that caused me pain. I bandaged the wound tightly, focusing on the act, not the confusing feelings stirring within me.

"Why did you do this?"

I glanced into Philip's eyes. "Because you might die from infection."

He waved my answer away. "Why do you care?" When I didn't reply, he added, "I thought you realized that you only kissed me out of curiosity and boredom."

"You're still my friend—"

"Nonsense," he cut me off. "I don't believe you. I think you care more than you are comfortable to admit, which scares you. You don't believe we can be together because of your father."

Frustration bubbled up in me, overshadowing my need for denial. "Yes," I gritted out. "We can never be together, so we might as well make this as painless as possible, instead of torturing ourselves." I turned on my heels and stormed to the opposite side of the boat. Clutching the rail tightly, I stared out over the water as stupid, unstoppable tears flowed from my eyes.

❧ 26 ❧

CLARA

After our dispute, Philip and I didn't speak until the sailboat reached the grotto. It wasn't hard for me to locate the cave; an invisible energy was pulling me toward it, calling me to come closer. Biscuit too was attuned to the magic, throwing her mane this and that way and stomping her hooves the closer we got.

Once we reached a shallow spot, Philip dropped the anchor and helped Biscuit and Ace out of the boat. He stretched his arm out for me as well, but I refused his aid, jostling my own way through the hip-deep water. The cave was large enough for the horses to fit, so we guided them inside. I expected to see a trap or a wild animal waiting for us, but there was nothing in the cave besides a big chasm in the middle under which was ocean water. Even if we fell into it, we would be fine as long as the current wasn't too strong.

"Do you still think this is the place? Because if not, we should find a way out of this realm before Leon finds us," Philip said as disappointment swirled in me.

Had I misjudged the grotto? Was the trinket we were supposed to collect somewhere else? I studied the water carefully, making out multi-colored fish, corals, and seahorses. "Maybe we need to talk to one of them."

Philip moved closer and touched the surface with his hand. "How? We can't be underwater and talk."

"No, we can't. But perhaps one of them can talk outside of the water." Just then a tall, gray fin swam toward us, moving side to side. Its ugly head popped out of the water, and it opened its mouth, revealing countless sharp teeth. A shark.

Philip pushed me behind himself, but I stepped around him. I couldn't let this chance slip through my fingers. "Are you the magical guardian in this kingdom?"

The shark huffed, and his foul breath, which was a mixture of dead fish and seawater, hit me.

"We're on our way to the Inverse Kingdom to break a curse that has been cast over me. If I don't break the curse by feeding the Crackatook to the nutcracker, I will turn into a wooden doll." When there was no response, I added, "We need your help to succeed against the seven-headed Mouse King."

The shark opened his maw again, and this time, a low voice droned through the cave. "Fetch me the clam with the pearl, and I'll help you." He swam away, and we dared to take a step closer to the water and look into its depths. I could see the clam all right, a white, round pearl glinting in the center of it. I didn't know how to dive, but that wasn't the main problem—the countless jellyfish surrounding it were. They were the colors of the rainbow and ranged from the size of a fist to that of an arm. I was certain some of them were poisonous.

As I tried to figure out a way to snatch the pearl without getting into the water, Philip took off his shirt and trousers, remaining only in his underwear.

"No!" I reached out for Philip, but he was too fast. He

dove into the depths of the ocean, toward the sandy bottom. I cried out as the jellyfish attached themselves to every inch of his body.

"He's very brave," the shark said. Even in the water, I could see that red bubbles appeared on Philip's skin as he shoved away the jellyfish and grabbed the shell.

"Hurry!" I screamed as Philip swam upward. His head broke the surface, and I grabbed his shoulder, pulling him out of the water. His eyes fluttered shut, and his skin was covered in blisters, his body burning up. I pushed him onto his back, feeling for his pulse. It was there, but weak.

The shark clicked his maw, and I quickly opened Philip's palm and put the shell with the pearl down onto the ground, afraid the shark would bite off Philip's hand to get it.

"We held up our end of the deal. Where is our reward?" I said with as much strength as I could muster while I prayed to whoever was listening, *Please don't let Philip die.*

The shark dove only to return a second later. He spat a ball of seaweed next to me. "Throw this onto your enemy. It will wind around him or her. Magical alga is difficult to cut through." With that, the shark dove into the ocean.

Since I had no antidote to remove the jellyfish venom from Philip's system, we would have to wait for it to leave naturally. In the meantime, I needed to get us out of the grotto before Leon found us. I made Ace kneel as low as he could, hauled Philip's motionless body onto him, and used Philip's belt to tie him to Ace's saddle. Then I brushed Biscuit's mane. "Please, find the portal."

Her neigh was a continuous low murmur as she pointed her head toward the entrance of the cave.

"No, not the boat," I said. "The portal isn't there. It's here."

"That it is. Too bad you won't have the option to open it or enjoy your engagement party."

I whirled around to be greeted by Leon's bright smile. It didn't seem charming any longer; it was fake. And his face was no longer handsome, but too sharp, too perfect, too devoid of humanity.

"Did you really believe you could escape without me noticing?" Leon's haughty tone made it clear he didn't think so. "You should have hidden, rather than gone to the most obvious location."

To gain time and come up with a plan, I played along. "Why did you show me the cave on our catamaran trip if you didn't want me to know about it?"

He rolled his eyes. "There's magic here. There's nothing I can do to stop a boat from being pulled toward it."

"Especially because you have magic in your blood."

He nodded with a proud smile, as if I had solved a puzzle.

"Why wait for me here? Why not ambush me earlier or put me under your spell back at Schönbrunn?" As I talked, I casually brushed against Philip, removing a tiny blade from his belt's holster.

Leon smirked, still confident he had the upper hand. "I did spike your drink in Schönbrunn the night we met. But the draft was too weak since too much time had passed from it being cooked. The brew is strongest here when it has just been made." He shrugged. "But it all worked out in the end. Unlike the other princes, who thought you useless, I saw your competence. I expected you to try and break the curse. All I had to do was intercept you at the right moment. Simon, who has as much self-control as a pig, was no competition. Julian could bore even the most patient maiden to death and was clueless when it came to the real world and not his books. Felix was my only competitor. His plan was respectable but didn't cut it in the end."

"How did you know about the curse and that I had to

travel through your kingdom?" I clutched the blade tightly, reassured by its cold, smooth surface.

He puffed his chest out. "I paid good coin to have eyes and ears everywhere in the palace and in Gumpoldskirchen. The pixie was very talkative."

Bile rose in my throat. Even though I had known for quite some time that Leon had tricked me, the extent of his betrayal still stung.

"Your tenacity impresses me," Leon continued cheerfully, as if we were friends and this was a polite conversation. "But too much of anything isn't good. That's why you'll have to wait out our engagement and marriage ceremony with a spell binding your free will."

He reached for something in his pocket, and I stormed toward him. A black vial flashed in his hand as I jammed the knife into his neck. He roared in pain, his eyes bulged, but he didn't drop the vial. Instead, he uncorked it.

He was much stronger than me, but I had the benefit of facing the water. Channeling all my anger, I shoved him full force into the ocean, breathing a sigh of relief as the waves engulfed him and the black vial.

A second later, his face came back up; he was fighting the current, swimming toward us.

I gasped and mounted Biscuit. "Now, please!"

Biscuit stooped low in front of the cave's abyss. At first, it appeared as if she was about to drink the water, and I almost stopped her, but then she pressed her horn against the turquoise surface, which transformed into a swirling blue archway.

"The portal can't be down there," I whispered, terrified of drowning or being carried away by a strong current.

Biscuit neighed impatiently as sloshing sounds came from behind me. Leon had made it out of the ocean. I had to choose between trusting Biscuit or allowing Leon to take me prisoner. I gave Ace a hard shove, and he dropped into the portal. Biscuit and I followed suit.

Leon cursed behind us, but his voice was soon cut off by the whooshing sounds that engulfed me as I traveled through the portal.

Out on the other side, I discovered with relief that I had stayed magically dry, and more importantly, that the portal had closed behind me, making it impossible for Leon to follow me until it was reopened.

"What happened?" Philip's eyes were at half-mast, his torso leaning heavily on Ace.

"We got the third trinket. A seaweed binding that is hard to cut through."

Philip shivered, probably an aftereffect from the jellyfish stings. "You were right. We had to go to the grotto with Biscuit and Ace to escape Leon's kingdom, but I still wish we hadn't used up the gift of paralyzation." He paused for a beat, scrunching up his forehead. "Did Leon catch up to us? I thought I heard his voice."

"Yes." I looked at the spot where the portal had been. "We should hurry in case he manages to reopen the portal."

The nutcracker in my purse chimed and spoke in his eerie voice, which I had learned to despise so much, "Only one more day remains. If you don't solve the curse, you'll turn into a wooden doll and your soul will be locked for all eternity inside of me."

"My time is up," I whispered, hopelessness engulfing me.

❦ 27 ❦

GRISELDA

Back when I had been on Snake Island, I had hated my life, dreaming of belonging somewhere important, instead of being surrounded by misfits, dreaming of being in control and in charge. When I had reached the Inverse Kingdom, I had believed I was a finger's breadth away from my goals. But since meeting the Mouse King, I hadn't felt even an ounce of control or power. Instead, a familiar rage consumed me, spiking every time he commanded me around, every time he told me I wasn't good enough.

"Don't slump forward, Griselda."

"You messed up the traps, Griselda."

"Do I have to show you again, Griselda?"

Each admonishment made me flinch and ball my fists. I could take specific critique, but he didn't just attack what I was doing but also who I was. The Mouse King chipped away at me, one word at a time.

"You're good for nothing, Griselda."

"How will you ever be an empress with your lack of manners and skills, Griselda?"

"The emperor should have executed you, Griselda, not your mother. She would have been more useful."

The last phrase always hurt the worst, not because the Mouse King told me that the world would be better off with me dead, but because that's how my mother had made me feel. I had been her burden. I had made her life more difficult. If not for me, her mouse shifter secret wouldn't have been discovered, and she wouldn't have been executed.

Despite voicing his misgivings about my shortcomings and lack of skills, the Mouse King tasked me with setting all the traps for Clara. "Stand here." He pointed at a corner. "Don't do or say anything while I think. I need to focus."

When he looked away, I rolled my eyes and inched toward the wooden shelf where a golden nut lay in an intricate bronze egg cup.

"Don't touch it," the Mouse King snarled, even though I had made no move to reach for the Crackatook.

Knowing that asking questions about it would only arouse his suspicion, which might lead to him deciding he didn't need me and killing me, I stayed quiet while the Mouse King alternated between pacing and scribbling something with a quill.

"Right. I have made a decision," he pronounced grandly, and I straightened my spine. "I will stay here with the Crackatook while you enhance the castle's natural tricks, so that Clara has no chance of reaching this room." I nodded, and he continued. "I'll tell you what to do for each station, working our way backward from my throne room and starting with the soldiers. Understood?"

"Yes," I said quickly, and immediately realized he had made a foot soldier out of me. I was in his shadow just the way I had been in my mother's shadow growing up.

"Instead of doing target practice and fighting each other, the soldiers will face the way Clara will enter." I nodded my understanding, but his arm lashed out, backhanding me. "What are you standing here for? Go, do your first task. I need to be alone to come up with the rest. I can't think while being distracted."

I scurried out of the room, my nostrils flaring, my body pulled taut with tension.

It took the toy soldiers what felt like months to grasp that they all had to face the direction of the corridor, from which Clara would come, and shoot their guns incessantly. The door to the corridor would remain open so that they could spot my stepsister sooner. Of course, the time it took me to teach the soldiers was attributed by the Mouse King as me being daft, and not the toy soldiers being toys without brains.

My next task proved much easier. Since the ballerinas had cut off the old rope, I had to replace it with a new one so I could set all the traps. I would then remove it once I was done with my duties and rejoin the Mouse King, making it impossible for Clara to cross into the king's quarters.

"What's next?" the Mouse King quizzed.

"The staircase, but I don't think we have to do anything there." I didn't think there was any way that a nonmagical, naive girl like Clara would figure out that she should use the banister instead of the stairs to reach the top.

"Do you want to remain a dolt your whole life?" The Mouse King's seven pairs of eyes flamed with anger, and each of his seven foreheads sported a throbbing vein. "Doing the bare minimum is what kept you a darn prisoner for ten years! Winners fight, plan, and always prepare for the worst outcome! No one can be trusted." As he spoke, he flailed his arms wildly, and I stepped back, not eager to receive another slap.

"After you set up the other traps, on your way back, you will put barbs along the railing." The Mouse King thrust a box with barbs and tar-based glue into my hands, and I accepted it meekly, hating him for intimidating me and myself for cowering.

"And take this. To spot this Clara when she comes through." He shoved binoculars into my hands, then rattled off the rest of his commands. As soon as he was done, I ran off to perform my tasks, eager to get away from him. I checked on the soldiers, who were facing the right way and told them not to shoot me, then crossed the new rope, attaching one end myself and making the ballerinas attach the other one. They didn't seem too eager to help, but when a guard dropped them a letter from the Mouse King to be read, their snarls turned into tight faces and they assisted me immediately. I didn't ask what he had threatened them with, simply moved on to my next chore, which was to rile the ballerinas up and make them more vicious than ever. This was by far the easiest thing to do. After spending days in the Mouse King's company, I was a ball of rage and enjoyed channeling my aggression, which was freeing and made me feel ten pounds lighter, at least for a little while.

"Don't stand around, you useless geese!" I put my fists on my hips. "You must prove your worth; otherwise you'll all be thrown into the boiling lake."

My words whipped the ballerinas into action as they probably imagined the pain and horror of their wooden bodies cooking in the boiling lake. They performed jetés and twirled around me, each move sharp and deadly. I had no doubt they would rip Clara limb from limb with pleasure.

If it had been up to me, I would've left the hedge maze alone. After all, avoiding the electrical jolts from the criss-crossing lines of light was impossible.

Even on the unlikely chance that Clara avoided being electrocuted, she would be hit by a sleep-inducing mist, which even I hadn't escaped, and which I was certain would be the end of her. The Mouse King, however, didn't think this was enough, so I repositioned the sleep-inducing misters in the most efficient way, making sure they sprayed her as much as possible.

Ten minutes after I had finished, the messenger toy soldier handed me a letter with two lines.

Well done. Now move on to the boat.

I groaned, realizing the Mouse King must've been watching my progress through his own set of binoculars and that I wasn't as free as I hoped to be. Yet, a part of me felt pride, gobbled up the praise, and stored it away into my memory to be retrieved later when I needed it.

The moment arrived much quicker than I anticipated since my next task, the wooden boat, refused to be destroyed. I tried everything, weighing it down with stones, tearing it apart, setting it on fire, but nothing damaged the magical object. My efforts to keep it by the castle failed too. It wouldn't stay on the shore. No matter how much I tried to tie it down, it always sailed back out into the lake, making me chase after it and burn my feet, ankles, and calves as the boiling water seeped through my leather boots.

When the messenger delivered my next letter, he didn't make eye contact.

If you can't destroy the boat, you imbecile goose, make it the danger.

I reread the line several times, each word a punch in the sternum. How would I make the boat the threat? What would the Mouse King do to me if I failed?

For a long time, I stood there, sifting through possibilities. Finally, I came up with a plan and whistled for the messenger. "Bring me acid, the king's snake, and animal traps."

He returned minutes later, and I coated the inside of the boat in a thick acidic layer, which burned through the thick gloves I wore, eating away at the skin on my hands. Then I put in two animal traps and the basket with the snake, removing the lid. The combination of the acid, traps, and snake would at least injure Clara and hopefully make her panic enough to jump into the boiling water where she would be cooked within minutes.

When I was done with the boat, I wiped the sweat from my face, accidentally rubbing some acid into my forehead, which set my skin on fire. I hurried to the flaming entrance and let the cooling water wash over me, not daring to let out a cry of pain, knowing it would demonstrate to the Mouse King how weak I was and attract the ballerinas, which fed on fear and misery. In their deranged state, they might easily mistake me for Clara and rip my arms out. Thus, I curled up into a ball on the ground, tucking in my tail and whimpering as quietly as I could until the burning sensation became bearable, hating myself. I bet Delilah wouldn't have messed up like that. What mischief was she up to now that she had the mirror? Was she spying on her brother? I shivered as I imagined what would happen if Delilah managed to escape prison. I only wanted my social standing back and to punish those who had harmed me. Delilah would harm people just for pleasure, of that I was certain.

Instead of returning to the king, I remained in my hiding spot. After everything, I needed and deserved a break, a moment to myself to gather my thoughts. I never got the chance.

A spot across the river shimmered, the air around it swirling. I held my breath. Was the portal opening? Was it really time? Or was it just a mirage caused by my exhausted mind?

When a girl with a long, thick braid galloped through the entrance on a beautiful snow-white unicorn, I could no longer deny that it was time to face my stepsister. She was followed by a young man on a simple black horse. He looked about her age and his upright posture and watchful gaze made me guess he was a soldier or a guard.

I pulled out the binoculars the Mouse King had given me and zoomed in on Clara, my heart doing a leap. *Clara*. She was finally here. As she glanced around, taking in the Inverse Kingdom, a plethora of memories flooded me.

Me and Clara playing. Clara offering me the prettiest doll, saying she didn't mind, that we could take turns playing with the new toy. Clara allowing me to borrow her pink velvet dress, even though she hadn't had the chance to wear it yet.

The memories of her kindness and innocence barreled into me like an avalanche I couldn't escape. The last memory gripped me hard.

On the floor in the playroom in the castle, I cried, repeating over and over, "I'm sorry, I didn't mean to do that." I had transformed back into my human form, but the emperor looked at me as if I was still a mouse, a rodent that disgusted him.

"How dare you!" My mother threw herself across the room at Clara, gripping her throat and choking her.

Immobilized with terror, I watched as Mother tried to throttle Clara and was subsequently pried off by the guards and shackled.

"You have attacked my daughter. You will be executed for this," the emperor said in a cold voice then turned to me. "And you will be exiled."

I sobbed as my mother was taken from the room and tried to follow her, but the guards blocked my way. I threw myself to the ground and became hysterical, my arms and legs flailing and kicking, gasping for air that didn't enter my lungs.

An arm came around my shoulder, comforting me. I looked up into Clara's blue eyes. "It's going to be all right," she promised. "I won't let him take you. I will protect you."

I pushed her away and snarled, "I don't need your help. You killed my mother."

"I didn't," she stammered. "She attacked me."

"I wish she would've finished you," I hissed, and Clara flinched.

The memory disintegrated, and I tumbled back into the present. I had to readjust the binoculars to find Clara and her guard, who were trying to get into the boat without sustaining burns. Clara kept glancing to her unicorn, whispering something. It was clear that she was reluctant to leave her unicorn behind. However, there was no way she could get her unicorn aboard. It was better that way. If the unicorn stayed on shore it would be safe.

With the Mouse King watching from his tower, I couldn't stay to see whether Clara failed or succeeded in her first trial. I needed to finish all my chores or risk my head being chopped of. Putting the barbs on the staircase railing would take up at least an hour. I needed to hurry and do my best to deliver Clara to her death. The realization that my enemy was about to die should've filled me with glee. Instead, I was overcome by an endless gulf of emptiness and numbness.

28

CLARA

I stared at the bubbling lake and the castle set in the middle of it, a sense of hopelessness overcoming me. When the ball of yarn had fully unrolled and Biscuit had tapped her horn against the portal with ease, I was overjoyed. But now that I was in the Inverse Kingdom, I wasn't sure I was ready to face the Mouse King and steal the Crackatook.

The scorpion, the fox, and the shark, as well as the princes, had been worthy adversaries, but somehow, I didn't think they were even half as bad as the Mouse King. How was I supposed to win against someone who had seven heads to anticipate every of my moves?

Knowing panic was not my friend, I shoved it down, telling myself I needed to succeed. Not just for myself, but also for Philip, for my father, for my dead mother, who had exchanged her life for mine, and for all the guards who were out there searching for the princess who had run away and whose heads were on the line if something happened to me.

I dismounted Biscuit and led her to the boat, which was big enough to hold her and Ace. "We need to bring them aboard."

Philip glanced incredulously from me to the horses. "How?"

"I don't know," I replied honestly. "But I'm certain they're meant to accompany us and help."

"All right," Philip said. "First, let's get the boat closer to shore."

I glanced from his hands, which had just healed from the jellyfish bites, to the burbling water. "You've done enough already, let me do this."

"Don't worry, there will be plenty to do for everyone." With a smile, he pulled two thick ropes from his saddle back and wound the end of both ropes around an anchor.

"Where did you get this?"

"I brought the anchors from Schönbrunn. Figured they would come in handy. Even though, I didn't expect to use them for a boat. I thought we might have to climb up walls." He swung the rope like a lasso. It flew in an arc, the anchor landing with a thump in the boat. Philip hauled the boat ashore and pulled on Ace's reins. "Get on board." Ace huffed, not moving a bit.

"Come on, Biscuit." I guided her toward the boat. She neighed and shook her head. "Please. We need to do this."

As Philip and I coaxed Biscuit and Ace aboard, the water gurgled and splashed us, burning our arms and legs. Finally, everyone was aboard, and I smiled at Philip. This journey was hard and challenging, but I would be fine because I had him. He was next to me every step of the way, providing continuous support and reassurance. He wasn't just my friend or a boy I had feelings for, he was my partner, someone I relied on and trusted. The comforting moment didn't last long as my feet began to tingle in an unpleasant way. The adrenaline left me and understanding sank in as I stared at my boots and their thinning soles. "The boat is coated in acid. We need to get onto the horses," I said. "They have metal shoes. They'll be fine."

"But how will we row?" Philip asked.

"We'll figure it out. Get on Ace." I couldn't watch Philip sustain more injuries.

We were in the saddles when the wind picked up, carrying our boat slowly but steadily across the lake.

I exhaled. "Well, at least the Inverse Kingdom is helping us to get to the castle."

Deep wrinkles formed on Philip's forehead. "I don't think it's doing it out of kindness. I think it's all part of the game. Since we've entered this realm, we were meant to reach the end. The realm doesn't care whether we die or live, only that we finish the game."

A shiver overcame me at his words. I didn't push it away, but I also didn't allow it to consume me. Taking Philip's hand, I said, "We have each other. We won't die. We will live."

He nodded in agreement, and we basked in this moment of reassurance until a hissing came from the corner. I gasped as I took in a tall lidless basket, a thick white-and-yellow snake rising out of it. A snake on its own was scary enough, but this snake kept growing and growing in front of my eyes until it was the size of a dragon. It pushed out its long, blood-red forked tongue that was the size of my face, and my heart beat violently in my chest, my breaths turning shallow.

"We can take her," Philip said and jumped off Ace. The snake charged, as if to disprove his sentence.

Biscuit threw her front legs up, and Ace backed up, swinging his tail wildly until there was a snapping sound, and an animal trap clamped shut around his tail. Terror flooded me. How could I free him and kill the snake? What else was on this boat?

Philip brandished his sword at the reptile, going for her

neck. Her tail hit him full force in his abdomen, and he tumbled to the ground, losing the weapon, which fell out of his reach. The snake charged, going for Philip's neck. I jumped off Biscuit and grabbed the sword. There was no time for me to throw it to Philip. I had to do this myself. With the snake focused on Philip, I was able to get close to it without her noticing me. I brought the sword down on her neck. It hit its mark but not deep enough. The snake hissed and retreated. I attacked again, but this time, I missed and the sword got stuck in the wood. I pulled with all my strength but couldn't get it out. The snake charged me. Weaponless, I backed away, desperately glancing around for anything I could use to kill the beast and end the fight before the acid burned through my boots and destroyed my feet. I stumbled against something sharp and hard—my salvation. I pretended to continue inching backward, but at the last second stepped to my right, allowing the snake to go right into the second animal trap.

The trap snapped shut. The snake's struggle drove the barbs deeper into her leathery skin, slashing her apart.

I turned to Philip, who had yanked the sword out of the boat. "We need to help Ace." While I kept the horse still, Philip cut off a chunk of his tail, the only way to get him out of the trap. The snake was still fighting her trap, but her struggle became feebler the more blood gushed from her wounds.

"I'm impressed." Philip gave me a lopsided smile. "By the time we return to Schönbrunn, you won't need any guards. You'll be able to protect yourself."

"Thank you." His warm words made me a head taller, and for the first time, I didn't think of my curse as a punishment, but an opportunity to grow.

I remounted Biscuit, trying as best as I could to ignore

the searing agony in my soles and the red blisters that covered them.

The boat reached the shore. The gray brick castle stood tall and imposing in front of us. What secrets and snares did the walls hold? Whatever they were, I was prepared to face them head-on. I had come too far to turn into a lifeless doll.

29

CLARA

Philip and I reached the castle, sustaining a few more burns from the boiling water, but not encountering any other trouble. Since no one was guarding the entry, we walked into the courtyard where we were greeted by a hedge maze.

I took out my bag and studied the remaining vials. "I still have the arctic fox's chameleon power and the shark's seaweed. But I don't think we can use either to figure our way out of the maze."

Philip shook his head. "No, we'll have to do this one without any help."

We stood quiet for a moment, considering what the best strategy was.

"The maze is most likely enchanted. I have no idea how magic works. I don't have magic in my blood." Philip glanced at me expectantly.

I shrugged and held my hands palms up. "I don't have any magic either."

Philip indicated Biscuit. "Perhaps she knows what to do."

I nodded. "All right, Biscuit, let's do this. You and I will work together and take care of each other so that we won't get lost in there forever and die from insanity, right?"

As a sign of her agreement and cooperation, Biscuit pushed her muzzle into my hand. Taking comfort in her and Philip's presence, I guided her into the maze. She trotted slowly and cautiously, choosing the path to the right. After seven steps, we were given the choice to either continue straight or turn to the left. When Biscuit didn't move, I said, "I think we should go straight ahead."

"Sure," Philip agreed.

We trotted forward, and a whooshing sounded behind us. When I pivoted around, I discovered a tall metal wall had fallen behind Philip and me, blocking off the path we had come from. In front of us, a maze of red lights crisscrossed from one hedge to the other. "I don't understand." I glanced at Philip who frowned.

"I have the feeling that we're supposed to avoid touching the lights."

"But that's impossible. Especially for Biscuit and Ace." I paused, then asked, "What do you think will happen if one of us hits the light?"

Instead of replying, Philip moved forward and touched a line. His body jolted, as if lightning had struck him, and he jerked back.

I swallowed hard. "We can't do this to Biscuit and Ace. We have to get through the maze on our own."

"But what if we need them in the castle?"

I shook my head. "It doesn't matter." I petted Biscuit. "Don't worry, I'll come back for you." She neighed and shoved her muzzle against Ace's saddle. "What?" I had no idea what she was trying to communicate. She bit the saddle and tugged on it, as if trying to take it off.

"I think she wants us to take it," I said.

"Why?" Philip asked.

"I don't know, but I'm sure she has a good reason."

"Very well." Philip took off the saddle. "It will be harder to get through the maze with this, but it's worth it if Biscuit is right and it will help us."

Slowly, we made our way between the light lines, jumping and crawling past them. Philip carried the saddle, which unfortunately didn't protect us from the lightening. A sweet mist sprayed from above. I glanced upward, feeling light-headed. "What is this?" My hand almost touched a line, but Philip pulled me away and into his chest.

"I don't know, but it's messing with my vision, making everything blurry."

"It's like Leon's potions." I blinked, trying to focus. "We need to protect ourselves. Give me your sword." When Philip handed it to me, I cut off two pieces of cloth from the bottom of my dress and handed him one, then tied the other one around my nose and mouth.

Helping each other, we made it past the next few lines, sustaining only a few shocks.

The mouth and nose guard helped for a while but then became soaked with the mist, forcing us to discard them.

"I want to rest." I was bone tired, and the maze seemed never-ending.

"Me too. Perhaps we can lie down just for a minute."

Like I had done in Leon's castle. My mind jumped to attention. "No! We need to continue! We're stronger than the mist." I tugged Philip forward. My skin brushed a light line, and a jolt went through me. I welcomed the pain, allowing it to wake me up.

We made it past a few more lines, our struggle growing. My brain knew I needed to beat the maze, but my body was so tired and broken. Soaked with sweat, my clothes clung to me, my heart pounded in a strange rhythm, and my breaths were shallow. When there were only three light lines left, silent tears of relief ran down my face.

We crawled underneath the first line, several jolts slamming my back. At the second line, which was split into two, a high and a low line, I jumped, my soles sustaining a hit. The final line was rapidly moving up and down. There was no way to avoid it.

Next to me, Philip collapsed to his knees and went into a coughing fit. I handed him the refillable water skin, and he gulped greedily. His chest rose and fell heavily. If he received any more jolts from the front, his heart might give out. I needed to protect him.

"Hug me!" When he didn't do anything, I pulled him to his feet and put his hands around my torso. "Don't let go!" Before I could lose my nerve, I lifted the saddle and walked through the final light line. A burning ache seized me, as if I were on fire. *You can do this. You will do this. You won't die now.*

Clutching on to my need to survive, I stumbled out of the maze and onto the green grass, dropping the saddle. My knees gave out, and I hit the floor. I knew that should hurt, but all I could feel was the coolness of the grass, which lulled me into a merciful unconsciousness.

Dramatic classical music, heavy on the string instruments, and footsteps that were loud yet dainty awoke me. I pushed off the grass stalks that jabbed my cheek and shook Philip, whose eyes fluttered open.

"What...where?" he asked in a sleepy voice as the music and footsteps grew louder.

"I don't know. But something's happening. Get up."

Philip pushed upward, a grunt leaving his lungs. He wasn't ready to face our next trial.

A dozen ballerinas leaped and twirled their way toward me, their petite bodies and elegant moves in juxtaposition to the vicious glares on their faces. Even though they carried no swords or other weapons, I was certain they would annihilate me without a second thought. It would have been hard to fight them with Philip's help, but without him, I had no idea how I would defeat all twelve by myself.

The paralyzation potion would have come in handy at that moment, but since I had already used it, I needed to rely on something else—either the chameleon magic or the seaweed binding.

Deciding to use the arctic fox's chameleon weapon, I opened the vial and ate one of the fox's tail hairs then stuffed the other hair into Philip's mouth, certain the ballerinas wouldn't care that he could barely sit up straight, let alone fight.

The second part of the camouflage spell was to stand next to the spot I wished to blend into, but I didn't have time to pick one as a ballerina came straight for me.

A pop sounded inside of my head, and my skin tingled, like I had a rash. The first ballerina jumped at me, and I reflexively brought up my hands to shield my face, only for her to come to a stop a few inches away from me. She didn't attack me but tilted her head sideways, as if studying me. I glanced down on myself and was shocked to find that there were two layers to me, the outer one wore a tutu and pointe shoes, making me look like a ballerina, while the layer below was the real me.

Philip too had two layers to him. If this hadn't been a life-threatening situation, I would have laughed at him in a tutu, but I had no time for amusement. We needed to get away from the ballerinas while they were whispering, trying to figure out if we were allies or foes.

I surveyed my surroundings and found a dilapidated staircase. A tingle went through me, and I was certain the Crackatook was hidden on the upper level. Grabbing Philip's hand and the saddle, I pulled him toward the stairs, hoping Biscuit was right and the heavy piece of leather would come in handy.

I took a few steps up the stairs only to realize I wasn't getting anywhere. Why wasn't this working? Behind me the ballerinas were whispering, throwing suspicious glares at us. Desperate, I glanced around, my gaze falling on the railing covered with barbs. Why would someone bother making the railing, not the stairs, deadly? They wouldn't. Unless the railing was the real staircase.

I squeezed Philip's hand. "Jump into the saddle after me." His eyes were less glassy than when he had woken up, and he gave me a firm nod.

I put the saddle on the railing and jumped onto it. As soon as Philip slid behind me, the railing wrenched us upward. "Thank you, Biscuit," I whispered as the thick leather was hit by one barb after another.

"Get them! They tricked us!" the ballerinas yelled behind us, and I looked down at myself to discover the camouflage spell had run out.

Philip and I reached the top, the railing throwing us hard to the ground. Afraid the ballerinas would come after us, I pushed up into a standing position, wincing as my limbs creaked.

"Good thinking." Philip took my face in his hands. "Are you all right?"

"Yes. You?"

He nodded. "We need to continue before the ballerinas catch up." I peered down the corridor only to realize that besides an inch of floor in front of me, there was no floor. The corridor, which was supposed to connect us to the rooms on the second floor was missing, revealing a steep fall and the first floor underneath.

"You still got the other rope?" I asked, eyeing the marble columns on our side and across the abyss.

Philip nodded and pulled out the second rope and attached the anchor to it. He swung the rope like a lasso and threw it. His first few tries missed, the anchor only grasping air and never reaching the other side.

"You can do this." I put all my conviction into my voice.

Philip swung the rope one more time, and it finally landed on the other side, the anchor hooking around the marble column. He attached the other end to the column next to us, pulling the rope taut and testing it for stablity. "We're good to go."

I hugged Philip tightly, trying not to think too much about what would happen if one of us lost balance.

"I'll go first," Philip said.

I didn't mind, since I was certain Philip had more practice in this kind of thing and hoped to learn by watching him. He put one foot, then the other on the rope and held his arms out wide for balance.

My heart clenched, and my adrenaline spiked. The words "I love you" sprang to my lips, and I almost blurted them out. It was only the realization of how distracting these three words were that kept my mouth shut.

With each step Philip took further away from me, the background faded more and more until all that remained was him and the rope. When he crossed to the other side, the breath I had been holding whooshed out of me, and then I realized that it was my turn. My palms turned clammy, and I shook like a leaf.

"Take it slowly, you'll be fine," Philip yelled, motioning for me to make the first step.

I put one foot on the rope and spread my arms to the sides, mimicking Philip. Several seconds passed before I was able to force myself to put the second foot on the rope.

Fear gripped me hard, fighting my determination to succeed. Each step was a battle. Each tiny flutter on my part and gust in the air tightened my gut and brought me closer to death.

I pressed on, focusing on Philip's calm, determined face. His eyebrows furrowed, and his body tensed a second before he called, "Grab the rope!"

Next thing I knew, the rope swayed and tented, then collapsed. My arms and legs flailed. Somehow, I managed to grab the rope. I wrapped my legs around it, holding on for dear life as I swung like a pendulum in a circle. A glowering ballerina stood with a hunting knife on the side I had come from. Below me ballerinas were forming a pyramid, the one on top reaching for the rope.

With a new wave of adrenaline, I pulled myself up the cord, cursing my tutors for never working on my upper body strength. Philip hauled the rope up, helping me to get to the top.

Sweat ran down my body, my muscles strained and a corset wrapped around my throat as I expected a ballerina hand to grab my ankle at any moment. Instead, smoke filled my lungs and heat singed my feet. The ballerinas had set the rope on fire, giving me the choice to either burn or tumble to my death.

30

GRISELDA

I couldn't believe my eyes. Clara was a tiny, dainty thing, and yet she was exhibiting the strength of a warrior. She reached higher and higher with her hands, pulling up her legs again and again. When the ballerinas set the rope on fire, she continued the strenuous climbing, and the guard, whose name was apparently Philip, also never stopped yanking the rope up, up, up. The fascinating part wasn't what they were doing, or that they had thought to do it, but rather that they persisted in the face of adversity. Instead of panicking or falling into despair, they fought for their lives.

My belief that Clara was a helpless, spoiled, and naive princess shattered in that moment. I had to acknowledge that I didn't know who my stepsister was, but I was scared and excited to find out. The longer I watched Clara, the harder it was to justify putting the nutcracker curse on her.

I shooed away the guilt that overcame me, reminding myself that I had to report on Clara's progress to the Mouse King.

Knowing Philip was too preoccupied with Clara to notice me, I made my way freely from the shadows into the light, down the corridor, and through the toy soldiers' training room.

"Don't shoot," I said in a calm and authoritarian voice, striding past them into the king's dark and dank chamber. The smell of rot greeted me as seven pairs of eyes scrutinized me, and seven pairs of lips turned into hard, unyielding lines. "What do you have to report, mouse shifter?" seven voices asked sharply, and my back broke out in goose bumps.

"Clara and her guard are crossing toward the soldiers."

The Mouse King balled his fists, his nostrils flaring.

Before he exploded, I hurried to explain what had happened to justify myself and to transfer the blame onto my stepsister and her ingenuity. "Clara and her guard used the hooves of the horses to avoid most of the acid and guided the snake into one of the traps."

"You killed my most loyal soldier!"

"I didn't. It was Clara."

The Mouse King advanced and I hurried through my tale, hoping to redirect his fury, "Clara and her guard cleared the maze by working together and used their clothes to protect themselves from breathing in the sleeping gas. With a chameleon potion, they made themselves look like ballerinas, which allowed them to reach the staircase. They rode up the railing on a saddle to avoid the barbs. The guard had a rope to cross the floorless space. When I left to report to you, the ballerinas set the rope on fire, but Clara was climbing it, her guard helping her."

"And you stood there like a nitwit, doing nothing!" The king threw a goblet at my head.

I ducked, avoiding the object, and yet a pain shot through my temple, as if I had been hit.

"You useless, daft girl! How do you ever expect to be an empress when I have to tell you every little step?"

"I thought you wanted me to report the progress to you.

That's why I hastened to retun." My voice sounded tiny—just how I felt.

The king pushed out his seven heads like a cobra ready to strike. "You should have shoved the boy. That way they would both be dead." He pushed me so hard, I toppled backward and into the wall. "Go! You better hope they haven't crossed yet and you haven't ruined everything!"

I darted out of the room, imagining my hands taking a sword and embedding it deep into the heart of my enemy. But it wasn't Clara's or Philip's chest that I saw. It was the Mouse King's. I'd had enough. I wanted him dead.

You don't mean that. You won't be anything without him, a voice inside my head said. *You must endure whatever he does to you if you want to become* empress.

What if I didn't want to become empress? What if the price was too high? I pressed my nails into my palms, creating bloody half-moons.

You must. You won't be anything if you don't become empress. *You'll be just a poor prisoner, who has escaped, constantly on the run, constantly hiding. You won't have a castle. You won't have a kingdom. You won't have subordinates obeying you.*

No, I wouldn't. But was that really what I wanted? To rule a kingdom? Or was I chasing Mother's dream to become an empress?

I rushed into the toy soldier's training room to find Clara and Philip at the end of the corridor. As they entered the training room, the toy soldiers took notice and raised their guns just as I met my stepsister's gaze.

"Don't shoot," I called, strangely proud of Clara being able to defeat the traps I had set. She hadn't come all this way to be shot. Wait, what was I doing? Why was I helping Clara? I shook my head. I wasn't helping her. I simply wasn't ready for her to die yet. I had suffered for years, she didn't get to exit this world with a quick bullet to her heart.

The soldiers lowered their guns, and Clara and Philip made their way over to me. With each step she took, my stomach contracted harder and harder. My anger rekindled, and I imagined putting my hands around Clara's neck and choking her. I didn't care if Philip would slay me while I did so. In fact, I wanted him to do it. Death would be a relief from the never-ending pain, confusion, and emptiness my life was.

Clara opened her mouth, and I prepared a response to her tirade. But the name-calling never started. Instead, she calmly said, "Griselda, I thought we might meet you here. Thank you for holding back the soldiers."

Taken aback by her unexpected words, I couldn't reply for several seconds. My hands dropped to my sides, and my back relaxed, but then my fury returned—not as white-hot as before, but still burning brightly. I lifted my chin, excited to see the betrayal on her face when I said my next words. "I booby-trapped the castle. It was me who put acid, the traps, and the snake into the boat. It was me who repositioned the misters dispersing the sleeping spell in the worst possible way. I put the barbs on the railing. I worked the ballerinas into a frenzy." I smiled widely, showing her I didn't care what she thought of me. I didn't need her approval. I didn't need her to see me as good. I hadn't called off the toy soldier because of her, out of pity or mercy. I had called them off for my own benefit because I wanted to see Clara fail and watch as the Mouse King decimated her and her companion.

Clara nodded. "I'm sure you had your reasons for doing so. I'm grateful you intervened with the soldiers."

At first, I thought I had heard wrong. How could Clara be grateful? How could she accept all the horrible things I had done to her and her companion, nearly killing them?

She took out the nutcracker. "I know you're angry with me, Griselda. What my father did was wrong. His decisions to execute your mother and send you into exile were beyond harsh, and you have every right to be furious with us." She inhaled and pressed on. "Sending you to prison for your whole life for shifting wasn't right. You didn't choose to be a mouse shifter. I hope you understand that just as it wasn't your choice to shift, it wasn't my choice to panic when you shifted. I had no idea what was going on, and I didn't know that my scream would lead to you being imprisoned and your mother's death. I was only seven years old, too young to understand the consequences of revealing your secret. After the guards walked you out, I begged and begged my father to change his mind, but nothing I said helped. I want you to know that I fought for you. I truly did."

My vision blurred, and I wondered if I was about to pass out. It was only when something wet trickled down my cheek that I realized I was crying. How dare Clara make me cry? How dare she make me weak! "I don't need your pity or help." I hardened my voice. "I've broken out of prison, traveled to the Inverse Kingdom, and secured an alliance with the Mouse King. He will ensure that you and your father die, and then I will become the empress of Austria."

"Are you sure about that?" Clara tilted her head slightly. "Do you really think he will make you empress? It appears to me that he made you his lackey, giving you traps to set."

My hand flashed out to backhand Clara. She caught my wrist midair and pushed it down, her grip not hard enough to hurt me, but strong enough that I couldn't wriggle out of it.

"I don't expect you to let go of your anger toward me any time soon, but I've traveled very far and fought countless obstacles." She held out the nutcracker. "I think I deserve a chance to try and solve the curse before I turn into a wooden doll."

I stared between my stepsister and the nutcracker as memories engulfed me.

Clara comforting me when my own mother told me I would never amount to anything, that I had neither beauty nor smarts.

Clara comforting me when I fell off the horse and my mother told me to be less clumsy next time.

Clara telling me that wetting my bed didn't make me a disgrace as my mother told me, and that accidents happened sometimes.

Pulling myself back to the present, I nodded weakly. "If you want to solve the curse, you better hurry up because your time is about to run out."

Not wanting to see the gratitude I didn't deserve on her face, I pivoted on my toes and walked to the Mouse King's throne room. "Ready?"

"Yes," Clara and Philip said in unison, and I pushed the door wide open, trying to ignore the sadness their closeness elicited in me.

❧ 31 ❧

CLARA

Philip and I followed Griselda into a gloomy room with slivers of light coming through smudgy, tiny windows. The crooked board creaked underneath my feet, and a filthy dank smell filled the decrepit space.

"You brought them here, instead of killing them? How dare you?" the Mouse King boomed, his rage directed at Griselda, who had led us into his sanctuary.

Taking advantage of his momentary distraction, I surveyed the room and spotted the golden Crackatook nut in a bronze egg holder in the wooden shelf behind the Mouse King.

My gaze didn't escape the Mouse King. Seven heads with seven pairs of sharp teeth and red, furious eyes turned on me. He drew his sword and advanced, seven maws snapping, sharp teeth glinting. With his seven heads, he had a clear advantage and would be able to anticipate our moves, making it impossible for us to retrieve the Crackatook behind him. It was time to use the gift of the shark. I pulled out the seaweed and threw it at the Mouse King, praying it would work as it should. The alga wrapped around his body, binding him, and

he struggled to move. Philip and I rushed toward the Crackatook, only for me to discover I couldn't remove it from the
egg holder. I twisted the egg this way and that, but it
wouldn't come off. In the meantime, the Mouse King was
biting through the seaweed at an alarming speed.

Philip drew his sword. "I'll hold him off. Get the Crackatook and feed it to the nutcracker."

Desperate, I grabbed the Crackatook and slammed the
egg holder against the shelf. A piece chipped off the egg
holder, but the nut was still stuck in it. Perhaps it was best to
take them together, leave the castle, and figure out how to
separate them once we were out of the Inverse Kingdom. If I
hadn't run out of time by then.

I slipped the Crackatook into my invisible purse inside
my cloak's pocket and was about to voice the new plan when
teeth snapped at me, one of them biting my earlobe. I
shrieked and pivoted around to find Philip on the ground and
the Mouse King free of his binding, advancing toward me,
swinging his sword high. I ducked as metal clanked against
metal. Philip had jumped to his feet and parried the Mouse
King's blows, but he was at a disadvantage with the seven
heads snapping at him, the necks elongating like cobras. A
bite to Philip's wrist made blood sputter out of the wound
and forced Philip to release his blade, which clattered to the
floor. The Mouse King's sword arched through the air, aiming
for Philip's chest. I dived for his discarded sword and sliced
through the mouse neck closest to me. The head tumbled to
the ground and rolled, releasing an earsplitting screech.

The Mouse King whirled on me, his sword coming for my
chest. He was so quick, he would have speared me, if not for
Griselda, who kicked him hard in the groin, making him bend
over at the waist. She kicked him again, and his sword clattered to the ground.

"Cut off the other heads!" she yelled.

She didn't have to tell me twice. The second head rolled not a minute later, the distraction enough for Philip to take possession of the Mouse King's sword and chop off a third head. But just because the Mouse King was weaponless didn't mean he was helpless. His hand came around my throat and squeezed tight. I froze as blood rushed through my head, and my heart pounded, ready to jump out of my chest while memories of Griselda's mother choking me overcame me.

Griselda charged him, but he used his other hand to toss her with ease against a wall. From behind, Philip severed another head, and I finally regained control of my limbs and sprang into action. I bit hard into the Mouse King's forearm. His grip on my throat released momentarily, and I brought my sword down, cutting off his wrist, which spurted with crimson blood, then decapitated one more head.

Philip severed the final two heads, and the Mouse King collapsed. A flutter of relief rushed through me, but before it could settle in, a clock chimed, and the nutcracker's eerie, hopeless voice sounded. "Your time is up. You failed to break the curse. Your body will turn into a wooden doll while your soul will be captured inside of me for all eternity."

I pulled out the Crackatook. "We need to get it out of the egg holder." I tried to take a step toward Philip, only to discover my legs weren't working. My feet had already turned to wood, and now the transformation was creeping up my shins. *No, no, no. I was this close. I couldn't fail now.*

Icy fear settled in my gut, and I whispered, "It's too late."

Griselda rose from her crouch and stumbled toward me, her eyes wide with terror as my legs turned to wood. Philip stormed into action. He jammed his blade underneath the Crackatook until he separated it from the egg holder. I handed him the nutcracker and he shoved the nut into its mouth and pushed the lever. The nut split with a loud crack, and my hope returned for a second. But when I looked down at myself, I realized the curse hadn't stopped. My legs were wooden, and the curse was crawling up my hips.

"Why isn't it working?" Philip shook Griselda's shoulders. "You brought this on her. Solve it!"

She blinked rapidly, as if trying to get her shock under control, and then said, "Feeding the Crackatook to the nutcracker is the first part. You must take seven steps backward to stop the curse."

Unable to feel my hands any longer, I knew I had to make peace with the possibility of dying, and said, "I love you, Philip. I'll always love you."

His eyes welled with tears as he walked backward, not replying to my confession, but counting, "One. Two. Three. Four. Five."

My mouth became immobile, and I beseeched him with my gaze to tell me he loved me before I lost my ability to hear.

"Six. Seven." Philip's foot flew out from under him on his last step as he stumbled over one of the dead Mouse King's heads. With a loud thump, he landed on his back.

It was over. I closed my eyes as tears ran down my face. Wait, I could feel my face. I opened my mouth. "Philip?" I was able to speak. Seconds later, I could move my arms, my torso, and finally, my legs and feet.

"Philip!" I rushed forward, concerned he wasn't moving or making a sound. Certainly, the fall couldn't have been that bad.

"Philip? Philip! Are you all right?" My world stopped as I took in his face. It was motionless and wooden. I glared up at Griselda. "What happened?"

She folded her hands, not replying.

"What happened?" I demanded more forcefully.

"He broke the curse, but part of the curse was to take

seven steps backward without losing one's footing. Because he did lose his footing, the curse backfired on to him."

"What's the counter-curse?"

"There is none."

I shook my head, refusing to believe that. "Not that you know of. But I'll find one." Remembering Mr. Drosselmeyer's request for the seven-headed Mouse King's sword, I grabbed it and put it into my belt. "Help me carry Philip to Ace."

Griselda raised her eyebrows, as if wondering whether I was serious. I took Philip's shoulder to show her I meant business, and she lifted his legs.

"If you help me, I'll ensure that there will be a place for you in Schönbrunn."

Her mouth widened in an O. "Why?"

"Because it's the right thing to do. Because Schönbrunn was meant to be your home."

"But I cursed you, and now——" She hesitated. "——your friend is... changed."

"You also helped me with the Mouse King, and you helped Philip to lift the curse when I couldn't do anything." I wanted to reassure her that everything would be fine if she returned to Vienna, but I knew it wouldn't be an easy road. So, instead, I made a promise I could keep. "As long as I live, no harm shall come to you if you return to Schönbrunn. I understand if you don't want to, but know that you can always change your mind later. Just send a letter for me."

Griselda's chin wobbled. "Thank you, Clara."

We entered the toy soldiers' room, and she called, "Don't shoot. And bring us a ladder long enough to get to the first floor."

The soldiers did as she commanded, and a ladder was placed at the top of the second story, reaching to the first story.

"That's much better," I said, glad I didn't have to balance

on a rope again, not that that would have been possible while carrying Philip. Even with the ladder in place, my and Griselda's descent with Philip was slow and cumbersome. Each time a step creaked, my chest contracted, and with each passing second, the burn in my shoulders and arms increased.

We pressed on and eventually reached the ground.

The clicking of pointe shoes sounded, and the ballerina marionettes twirled toward us. I was about to lower Philip to the ground and pull his sword, but before I could, Griselda yelled, "Go away."

Miraculously, they listened.

"The ballerinas and toy soldiers take orders from you," I said, awed, and Griselda's cheeks colored at the praise.

She moved a few levers. The lights and mist in the maze vanished, and the metal separator lifted. Biscuit and Ace cantered toward us.

With Griselda's help, I heaved Philip on Ace, reminding myself that I wasn't doing so for the first time and that he had recovered before. This time, however, was different. This time, Philip wasn't just tired or ill. This time, he wasn't Philip anymore. Was his soul still within his body? Or was his soul inside the nutcracker? If so, was there a way to retrieve it?

Stop, I told myself before my mind could wander in circles. I wouldn't worry about this until I reached Gumpold-skirchen. Mr. Drosselmeyer would know what to do, and he would help me because I had the Mouse King's sword.

Before we went into the maze, Griselda fiddled around the bushes where I guessed the misters were positioned. Then she led me through the labyrinth and toward the boat, onto which she threw a heavy blanket. "It's impenetrable. It will protect you from the acid," she explained.

I guided Ace onto the boat and then returned for Biscuit. So focused was I on them, it was only when the boat moved away from shore that I realized Griselda wasn't in it.

"Jump in," I urged her, but she shook her head, a sad smile playing on her lips.

"Your offer is generous, Clara. But I don't deserve to return to Schönbrunn after all the misery I've caused. To the court and your people, I'll always be the daughter of the woman who tried to kill the princess, or the girl who cursed the princess. I want to stay here and start over, see if I can transform this destitute castle into something worthwhile."

I was so far away from her now that I had to scream to be heard. "I'm sure you will. But if you ever want to leave, let me know. And please write to me. I missed your company."

I wondered if my last sentence was too much, but then an answer as soft as a lullaby reached my ears. "I missed you too, little sister."

CLARA

On the other shore, we debarked the boat, and Biscuit tapped her horn against the portal, opening it. We galloped through it, leaving the Inverse Kingdom and returning to the forest, Ace and Philip following behind.

Thankfully, the end of the ball of yarn was still on the ground. Eager to free Philip from his wooden state, I pushed Biscuit and Ace hard, barely stopping to rest, eat, or drink. The thread seemed to continue forever, but finally, a sweet melody reached my ears and in front of me opened the Gumpoldskirchen village surrounded by a blue, glittering light. We had arrived. Just like last time, half a dozen griffins circled me. Even though they had allowed me to pass previously, a cold shiver ran through me at their menacing eagle claws, sharp beaks, and strong lion hindlegs.

"What are you doing here, human? You shouldn't be here. This is the magic folks' territory," the biggest griffin said.

I inclined my head in a respectful nod. "My name is Clara, Princess of Austria, and I've returned to Gumpoldskirchen to see Mr. Drosselmeyer and give him the sword he had asked me to procure." I unsheathed the Mouse King's blade and held it out in both hands in a nonthreatening gesture. "I also have come to seek his counsel for my friend." I indicated Philip's wooden form.

The griffin tilted his head and nodded a second later. "She speaks the truth."

"She speaks the truth," the five griffins echoed behind him.

"You shall enter and do what you came for," the leader said. "But as soon as you're finished, you must be on your way, human."

"I understand," I replied.

"Very well. You may pass." The griffins ascended, and I stepped into the blue light and through the barrier. On the other side, luscious grass and a cobblestone road greeted me. Awe overtook me at the tall trees, whose tops I couldn't see, and sheep-sized mushrooms, which grew in a spiral fashion. A group of dwarfs with hammers and heavy bags slung across their shoulders marched across the path, but this time, I didn't need to ask for their help, knowing where I was going. I strode past the pond, in which a mermaid splashed. Then I passed the wide tree with the pods on its branches, wondering whether it had been Daphne or another pixie that had betrayed the path of my journey to Leon. I shook my head. It didn't matter; it was in the past.

I stopped at the straw-roofed house with midnight blue windows and got off Biscuit. "Stay here," I told her and Ace, then knocked. "Mr. Drosselmeyer, it's me, Clara. I've returned."

"Come on in," a hoarse voice replied. I stepped inside the workshop, meeting Mr. Drosselmeyer's one good eye.

"You solved the curse, but you lost your companion," he commented calmly, not betraying any emotion.

"We ran out of time. The curse unfolded, and I was turning into a wooden doll. I couldn't separate the Crackatook from the egg holder, so Philip tried. He was successful and fed the nut to the nutcracker, then took seven steps backward but stumbled on his seventh step over one of the heads of the dead Mouse King. The curse backfired on Philip."

"I see." Mr. Drosselmeyer stroked his pointy white beard.

His casualness made me tense. "I need your help." I balled my fists to keep my hands from trembling.

"There's nothing I can do. It's not up to me to solve the curse."

I wanted to scream at him and stamp my feet, but instead, I produced the Mouse King's blade and held it out. "If you want the sword, you will help me." I clomped outside, hoping Mr. Drosselmeyer would follow me. Once he saw Philip, he would certainly understand how dire the situation was and help.

Mr. Drosselmeyer stared at Philip's wooden form and repeated, "I can't reverse the curse. There's nothing I can do."

I shook my head, refusing to believe that. "There has to be something you can do."

"I'm afraid not."

I put the sword into my belt and crossed my arms. "I won't give you the sword until you help me."

"The sword was payment for the magic ball of yarn, not for any future favors."

I stared at my feet, unable to meet his gaze. He was right; he had already paid for the weapon. Without the yarn ball, I would have never been able to find the Crackatook and break the curse. But couldn't Mr. Drosselmeyer see how important Philip was to me? How could he let an innocent man suffer? Mr. Drosselmeyer's lack of empathy was a stab in my gut, and yet it didn't give me the right to go back on my promise.

Reluctantly, I handed the sword handle first to him. "Please, if you know anything, tell me." I turned to Philip's unmoving form. "I can't live without you Philip. I love you. I need you. You're my friend, my confidant. I wouldn't be the person I am today without you."

The air around Philip shimmered. Tiny golden and silver dust particles moved around in a mesmerizing dance. Slowly, Philip's eyes gained depth and clarity. He blinked several times, as if waking from a dream, and then opened his mouth. At first nothing came out, but then he said, "I love you too, Clara."

Before I knew it, he had jumped off Ace. His arms lifted me by the waist and whirled me in a circle.

"I don't understand," I sobbed with joy.

"Only true love can break the spell," Mr. Drosselmeyer said. "I couldn't help you, Clara, because you had to do this yourself."

Once Philip put me down on the ground, I faced Mr. Drosselmeyer. "So, this is it? The curse is broken?" I pulled out the nutcracker. "He'll never be able to hurt me again?"

Mr. Drosselmeyer nodded. "The nutcracker is harmless. The curse has been put to rest once and for all, but that doesn't mean your journey is over. I understand that not many know about your relationship with Philip."

My elation nosedived. Father would never allow me to marry Philip. For the first time, I didn't care. I would return to Schönbrunn to let Father know that I was safe, but I wouldn't stay. I was done feeling guilty about who I was and trying to be someone I wasn't. I loved Father, but I couldn't sacrifice myself and become a shell of myself to make him proud.

I squeezed Philip's hand. "I'll abdicate my title to be with you."

His eyes welled with tears. "You can't. You're the only heir."

"Yes, I can. I'm sure Father will find someone else to

ascend the throne. I would rather be a happy nomad with you than be a miserable empress with a spouse I don't love."

"The situation might be not quite as dire as you imagine," Mr. Drosselmeyer said.

I gave him a polite smile, appreciating his effort to be optimistic, even though I doubted he was right, which was fine with me. For Philip, I was prepared to sacrifice my title, my kingdom, and my home. For him, I would stop chasing Father's approval and try to fill the void Mother's death had caused. It was horrible that she had died of the aftereffects of childbirth, but I had finally understood that no amount of self-flagellation would bring her back. As for my father, I hoped he could accept me the way I was and be proud of the real me, not a version he wanted me to be.

It was time to truly start living my life with Philip. I loved him. And he loved me. We had been through so much together on this journey, our feelings couldn't be undone. I would fight for us, no matter what it took.

❦ 33 ❦

CLARA

I stared at the wide, three story, butter-yellow Schönbrunn Palace, the fountains and gardens in front of it. The palace was the size it had always been, and yet, after my journey, it felt small. It was significant, but it was no longer the center of my universe now that I knew how much was out there in the world.

My stomach knotted. I was excited to see my home and fall around Father's neck, tell him everything was fine, that the curse was broken. But I hated that after delivering the happy news, I would have to disappoint him with my decision about my future. However, no matter how painful and tough this conversation would be, we needed to have it. I had to stay true to myself and my love for Philip. I couldn't marry any of the four princes or anyone else besides Philip. I could no longer pretend that my inquisitive and adventurous nature was something that could be trained out of me or would die down with time. This was who I was, and it was time for Father to either accept the real me or let me go.

As we rode to the entry, my heartbeat picked up. "We're

here. No backing out now." My voice trembled, and Philip intertwined his fingers with mine.

"We're in this together. Whatever happens, I won't leave unless you want me to."

"I don't." I disentangled my hand from his, not wanting the guards to know how my relationship with Philip had changed before I told Father.

Biscuit came to a stop, and I removed my hood. The moment the guards saw my face, their features widened with shock and recognition.

"I'm Princess Clara of Austria, let me through." My statement was unusually forceful for the old me but fit the new me that had survived in four hazardous magical dimensions.

Awakening from their stupor, the guards opened the gate, and one of them followed Philip and me inside.

The ladies and gentlemen in the courtyard froze. They gaped, then dropped into curtsies and bows. Some threw suspicious glances at Philip, others seemed warm, probably thinking him my savior. I wondered what they said about my disappearance. Most probably viewed it as a form of rebellion and didn't know that I had been cursed.

As soon as I dismounted Biscuit, a stable boy took her and Ace away. By now, four guards were around Philip and me. I gave them a long, hard look, making it clear that while they could accompany me, I was the one in charge.

With confident steps and a straight spine, I strode down the marble floors of the castle, taking in the beauty of the stained-glass windows, the sweet smell of cherry pie, and the giggles of the mischievous court. The comforting sense of home wrapped around my shoulders like a soft blanket. How I had missed it all.

Not asking the guards where the emperor was, I made my way to Father's study, certain that's where I would find him. Two of the guards darted in front of me, knocked on the door, and announced, "Princess Clara has returned, Your Majesty."

There was a pause, and then Father's low voice called, "Come in."

The double doors swung open, and I met Father's stern gaze that softened as he concluded that it was really me.

"Father!" I ran toward him and threw myself around his neck.

"You're alive! Thank God you're alive, Clara! You had me so worried! Why did you run away?" My father's steel eyes focused on me.

"I solved the curse. I couldn't just sit around and let the princes or the guards fight my battle. It was my mission, my problem."

"How could you expose yourself to so much danger?" Father shook his head slowly, looking me over. "Is it done? Completely?"

Just then there was a knock, and the door opened, the person not waiting to be called in. When white curls and a baby blue cloak came into view, I wasn't the least surprised. Only my godmother had the nerve to storm into the emperor's study.

I hugged her, and she whispered against my ear, "I knew you could do it."

Turning to Father, I said, "Let me tell you what happened." I summarized how I had found and entered the Gumpoldskirchen village, how Mr. Drosselmeyer had helped me, the four realms, and how the four princes sometimes on purpose and sometimes inadvertently had sabotaged me. I also highlighted the role Philip had played in all of this.

My recounting of the events at the Inverse Kingdom made Father's face turn red. "I'll find Griselda and ensure that her prison sentence in Snake Island will look like a holiday retreat compared to what's about to happen to her."

"She changed. She came through," I said, protecting my stepsister. "If not for her, I would be dead."

"That's true," Philip chimed in, speaking up for the first time during the conversation. "Griselda helped us to defeat the Mouse King. If not for her, I wouldn't have known to take seven steps backward to undo the curse. When I was a useless wooden statue, she helped Clara to leave the Inverse Kingdom."

Father's face lost some of his rage, but I could tell he was still thinking about punishing Griselda. I needed to sway his mind, so I said, "Please, Father, leave it. For me. This whole thing started with Griselda accidentally shifting. Just think about it, if things had been handled differently ten years ago, I would have never been cursed. We need to let it go. We can't continue this pointless fight. It must stop. Griselda has already extended an olive branch. She's helped me plenty. And she has suffered enough. She lost ten years of her life, and she lost her mother, the only family she had."

Father didn't reply for a long moment. Finally, he nodded. Knowing that was all I would get out of him, and that I couldn't expect him to be happy about my decision, I hugged him tightly before moving to the next topic.

"There's something else we need to discuss." My fingers tingled, and a swarm of bees nestled in my stomach. I knew I had made the right decision and that I couldn't marry anyone besides Philip, but I was scared of Father's rejection. It would slice through me. It would leave me parentless. And yet as much as it would hurt, I couldn't put this off. I took a deep breath. "The four princes," I began, "I can't marry them."

Father gave a tight smile. "Of course not. I would have never invited them to court you had I known what rotten characters they have." He rubbed his forehead. "I will arrange for different princes to court you." I opened my mouth, but he cut me off. "Naturally, I won't do so right away. I'll give you a few months, even a year if you want to recover from everything." In a sterner tone, he added, "But you need to understand, Clara, that you need a spouse. One day, I will be gone, and I can't bear the idea of leaving you alone to rule the kingdom."

I swallowed and gathered all my courage. This was it. This was the moment I'd been dreading and waiting for. "I'm not alone. I've already found someone."

Father's eyebrows shot up. Clearly, he had no idea who I was talking about.

Drawing more from my new-found courage, I took Philip's hand. "Philip has always been a dear friend of mine, but as we embarked on this journey, our feelings for each other changed and deepened. They are no longer just of the friendly nature." My voice quivered, but I pressed on. "I know he's not a prince, and not even part of the court, but I can't bear the idea of being with anyone else besides him. Please, Father, allow me to be with Philip. I promise I won't ask anything of you ever again. And if you want me to abdicate my title, I will. I understand that marrying him changes everything."

Godmother wrapped her arm around me. "Now, now, child, don't jump immediately to the gravest conclusion."

Father looked me over, as if I had grown wings or a tail, then he gave Philip an appraising gaze.

"You need to be checked by the physician, Clara." Father rang the bell on his desk. "I'll think about what you have told me. I'll give you my answer in three days."

My maid bustled into the room. Her cheeks sported a pinkish glow, and her big smile transformed her face into pure sunshine. "I'm so glad you're back, Your Highness." Iris curtsied before putting a hand on my upper back and guiding me away.

I shot a worried glance at Philip, afraid he would be

thrown into the dungeon while Father thought about his decision.

As if reading my mind, Godmother said, "Don't worry, I'll take care of him."

T hree days passed. During that time, I hadn't spoken to Philip, but he'd written me, telling me he wouldn't be able to see me until the ball to celebrate my safe return. The ball was scheduled for today and filled my stomach with hummingbirds. What if Father had ignored my wishes and invited more princes to this ball? What if he hoped that, in the midst of the pageantry, my feelings for Philip would fade?

And what about the court? Would they bombard me with questions about my journey? I doubted they would believe my answers or appreciate my unladylike behavior, but I didn't want to lie.

As all these thoughts raced through my head, Iris laced me up into a corseted golden dress with a big, poufy skirt. The exquisite gown was decorated with tiny crystals and featured low cap sleeves, exposing my collarbone. I wore elbow-length, white gloves, and my hair was put in a half updo, golden citrine crystals glittering in it. Upon seeing my reflection, I smiled before sadness overtook me. I wanted to be with Philip, I truly did, but I wished I didn't have to give up my relationship with Father, my home, and life as I knew it— the adjustment would be rough, especially in the beginning. Still, I was certain it was the right decision, and I was 100 percent prepared to go through with it.

A beautiful harp melody played as I entered the ballroom. The air was filled with the sweet smell of roses, and a sea of expensive gowns and gems greeted me. But my whole attention was directed on one person only.

Next to my father stood Philip in a fine navy suit with golden accents. I didn't know what it meant that Philip was by Father's side, but it sure seemed from their relaxed body postures that, while I had idled away most of the last three days alone in my room, they had spent a significant amount of time talking to each other. As soon as I reached them, Father gave me a hug and whispered, "You've made a good choice."

Before I could ask what he meant by that, Philip kissed my hand. I curtsied, getting lost in his deep, green eyes. How much I had missed them. How terrified I had been when the zest had gone out of them after the curse had backfired.

"I'm going to ask you a question," Philip said, only loud enough for me to hear. "I hope that's all right."

The trumpets sounded, and the harp music and dancing ceased. The whole court's attention zoomed in on me, Father, and Philip, and the heavy anticipation filled the room.

"You have been called here to celebrate the successful return of my daughter, Princess Clara," Father began. "But that is not all that there is to celebrate. Philip Hertzheim has been a wonderful member of the guard since joining us. He has gone above and beyond his responsibilities, and he has kept my daughter safe on her journey. Without him, my only child would be dead."

Father paused, and hushed whispers darted through the room as the court tried to figure out what was about to come. I was just as clueless as they were.

"Therefore, I have given Philip my blessing to wed my daughter, Princess Clara of Austria." This statement was met with a collective gasp.

I was too frozen to gasp or do anything. Philip dropped to one knee and asked, "Princess Clara, will you do me the honor and become my wife?"

"Yes, yes, yes!" Tears clouded my vision as a huge wave of joy overwhelmed me.

Philip slipped a pear-shaped diamond ring, which had been my mother's engagement ring, onto my finger and gave me a chaste kiss.

The room broke out into deafening applause, and the harps resumed playing.

"Thank you, Father." I embraced him tightly, happy tears rolling down my cheeks.

Father hugged me back. "Philip will be a good husband. He demonstrated his love and care for you on your journey. He also demonstrated ingenuity, quick thinking, and perseverance, all skills that a monarch needs."

"Thank you," I repeated through my tears.

"And you, Clara, showed fearlessness, ingenuity, and quick thinking. You will make a great empress one day."

More happy tears rose behind my eyes. Father hadn't just accepted that I wanted to marry Philip, he had finally accepted me the way I was.

Father released me. "Now go, enjoy your first dance as an engaged couple."

❧ 34 ❧

GRISELDA

THREE MONTHS LATER

The tawny owl circled above the maze seven times before she descended and dropped the long-awaited scroll with Schönbrunn's castle stamp into my hands. Upon closer examination, I realized there was a second scroll inside. I unrolled it to find a magnificent painting of Clara in her A-line wedding dress with a sweetheart neckline, which was decorated with tiny diamonds. An elaborate and blinding crown sat on her head, but even without it, anyone looking at the painting, would've immediately known she was a princess simply by the radiant way she held herself. Philip had been captured sideways, his attention fully on Clara, pure adoration in his gaze. Behind the overjoyed couple stood Biscuit and Ace, their heads inclined toward each other, as if they too were in love.

Tearing my eyes away from the painting, I read the letter.

Dear Griselda,

I hope you're well and that the castle renovations in the Inverse Kingdom are progressing nicely.

Please find enclosed a painting of Philip and me on our wedding day. It was simply perfect and truly the happiest day in my life. I am overjoyed that I get to live the rest of my life by the side of this wonderful man.

But enough about me, what is new with you? Last time you mentioned that you were planning to put on an event for mouse shifters in the Inverse Kingdom. How are the preparations coming along? And how are your dancing lessons going with the ballerinas?

I hope you're well and, as the Inverse Kingdom becomes more stable, you'll be able to sneak off and visit us. After my disappearance, I won't be able to leave my kingdom anytime soon, but I do hope to visit you in a year's time.

With warm wishes,

Clara

I rolled both scrolls back up and stuck them into the pocket of my satin pants. As it turned out, I preferred pants over dresses, and nature over a big court. I would've never fit into the traditional empress role my mother had coveted for me.

Finished with planting the amaryllis, I headed toward the ballerinas' rehearsal room. I remained at the door, not wanting to disturb them as they practiced new choreography, a combination of the classical ballet they knew and the polka that Clara had described in her previous letter, which was all the rage in Vienna.

Despite my efforts, my arrival didn't go unnoticed, and soon several of the girls waved at me, and I waved back, smiling. Ever since the Mouse King had died, the darkness that had lain over the Inverse Kingdom had broken. It had taken a few days, but eventually, the marionette ballerinas turned back into humans, and so did the toy soldiers. The water was no longer bubbling, and the fiery entrance had disappeared. The maze had turned into a fun place rather than a deadly one. Even the dank, dilapidated throne room was now filled with the sweet smell of hyacinths and aflush with sunlight. It had taken days to scrub away all the blood, dirt, spiderwebs, and treat the mold, but it was worth it.

And this was just the beginning. I planned to not only make the Inverse Kingdom my home but also that of all the mouse shifters in Europe. I wanted to create a place where mouse shifters could come together, a safe haven.

Leaving the ballerinas to their practice, I strolled outside and walked along the shore, contentment spreading in my chest. I had finally arrived. I was ready to live my life, ready to follow my dreams, ready to be happy. I was no longer living in the shadow of my mother. I was free of my hatred for Clara and the world. I was finally whole and at peace.

My gaze fell on the lake, which was so calm and clear that it mirrored my reflection.

I shivered, remembering the magic mirror I had left on Snake Island with Delilah. In the midst of everything, I had forgotten about it, but now, I wondered how much damage it could do in Delilah's eager hands. Would she use it to harm her brother? Had she already done so?

Swallowing hard, I decided to send my response to Clara that very night and warn her about the magic mirror. I clasped my hands together and said a silent prayer that the mirror would be taken from Delilah before anyone was hurt.

THE END

Dear Reader,

What a journey, right? I have always loved fairy tales, especially those that feature unicorns, griffins and other creatures. I grew up watching the Nutcracker, both the ballet and the animation movie, and adored both. That's why I was so excited to combine the Nutcracker with other fairy tales. I hoped you enjoyed reading it as much as I enjoyed writing it! The Nutcracker Curse is the first book in the Cursed Fairy Tale series. Book 2: The Bluebeard Curse will be released in mid-December 2018.

Have you ever read the Bluebeard fairy tale? The original story is very dark, and I've kept some of the gloomy touches while adding romance, magic, and plenty of twists and turns.

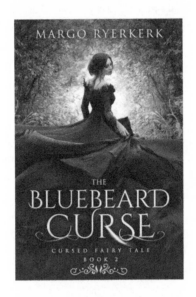

A devastating curse.
A broken soul.
A fearless girl.

After finding his sister crouched over their dead parents' bodies, Nolan turns her in. To cope with his crippling loss, he seeks to forget his sorrows in revelries. But trying to escape his life only creates more problems when two girls, last seen with him, drown.

Unable to bear the town's accusations, Nolan flees his home. Five years later, he's forced to return to the city that calls him

Bluebeard and accept his count title. His welcome is anything but warm, friends treat him with suspicion, and the worst is yet to come...

Jolie knows servants shouldn't interact with nobility, but there's something about Nolan Bluebeard that makes it impossible to stay away even if being close to him jeopardizes everything she has worked so hard for.

While Nolan desperately tries to rebuild his reputation with Jolie's help, a devastating curse has women around him falling dead one by one.

Will Nolan and Jolie break the curse, or will they die trying?

Preorder now and find out.

Thanks,

Margo Ryerkerk

P.S. When a reader writes a review, an author angel gets their wings.

Want more?

Sign up to my mailing list to receive The Fracture, a short story prequel for my YA Paranormal Ardere series and discover what events have shaped Gavin into the man he has become.

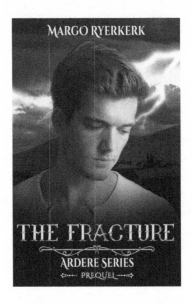

CLICK HERE TO JOIN MY NEWSLETTER
Or go to:
www.MargoRyerkerk.com/contact/

I will never share your personal details and will only notify
you periodically about new releases, sales, freebies, giveaways,
and bonus content.

ACKNOWLEDGMENTS

To my editors Virginia and Barbara—For their invaluable guidance and support.

To my cover artist Christian—For providing a gorgeous cover and willing to perform as many revisions as necessary to get it perfect.

To my alpha and beta readers at Scribophile—For the priceless feedback and helping me to become a better writer.

To my friends—For putting up with me, reading my early drafts, and allowing me to talk about my writing for hours.

To my family—For their patience and love.

To my husband Brian —For being my number one champion, for his love, unwavering support, and belief in me.

ABOUT THE AUTHOR

Margo Ryerkerk is the author of The Cursed Fairy Tale series and The Ardere Series, a YA paranormal series about magic, love, coming of age, and friendships. After completing a BS in Psychology, a MS in Marketing, and a two-years stint in the fashion world, she became a full-time author and can't believe she gets to spend her days creating stories. When she's not writing, she loves to read, travel, and dance to pop anthems.

Raised in Austria, Margo now lives in the USA with her husband and her Pomeranian.

Official Site: www.MargoRyerkerk.com
Facebook: Margo Ryerkerk
Goodreads: Margo Ryerkerk
Email: margoryerkerk@gmail.com
Twitter: @MargoRyerkerk
Instagram: MargoRyerkerk

ALSO BY MARGO RYERKERK

THE ARDERE SERIES

Fluidus Rising, Book 1

Mirror Sacrifice, Book 2

Spirit Snatcher, Book 3

Phoenix Call, Book 4

Made in the USA
Coppell, TX
21 December 2021

69866413R00135